THE HIDDEN PAST

The epic begins . . .

EPISODE I
THE PHANTOM MENACE™
By Patricia C. Wrede
Based on the screenplay and story by George Lucas

See Episode I through their eyes . . .

EPISODE I
JOURNAL

Anakin Skywalker
Queen Amidala

. . . and more to come

Before there was *The Phantom Menace*, there was . . .

JEDI APPRENTICE

#1 The Rising Force

#2 The Dark Rival

#3 The Hidden Past

. . . and more to come

STAR WARS

JEDI APPRENTICE

The Hidden Past

Jude Watson

LUCAS BOOKS

SCHOLASTIC INC.

New York Toronto London Auckland Sydney
Mexico City New Delhi Hong Kong

Cover design by Madalina Stefan. Cover art by Cliff Nielsen.

Scholastic Children's Books
Commonwealth House, 1-19 New Oxford Street, London WC1A 1NU
a division of Scholastic Ltd
London — New York — Toronto — Sydney — Auckland
Mexico City — New Delhi — Hong Kong

Published in the UK by Scholastic Ltd, 1999
Published in the USA by Scholastic Inc., 1999

ISBN 0 439 01447 6

1 3 5 7 9 10 8 6 4 2

Printed in the U.S.A.

THE HIDDEN PAST

CHAPTER 1

The marketplace in the city of Bandor was bustling as Obi-Wan Kenobi strode through it. He would have liked to stop to buy a piece of muja fruit, but Qui-Gon Jinn's steps never flagged. Obi-Wan's Master moved through the crowded streets with movements as fluid as a river. Without seeming to dodge or weave, he created a path with the least amount of energy. Obi-Wan felt like a clumsy sandcrawler next to a graceful starfighter.

He was careful to keep up. He was about to leave on his first official mission with Qui-Gon. The Jedi Knight had been reluctant to take Obi-Wan as his apprentice. Even though they had been through battles and adventures together, Qui-Gon had been hesitant. Only with their last adventure, facing death deep in the mining tunnels of Bandor together, had Qui-Gon made the decision to accept him as his apprentice.

Obi-Wan was still unsure of his Master's feelings about him. Qui-Gon was a quiet man who didn't share his thoughts until necessary. Obi-Wan knew little about the mission ahead. He would have to find the patience to wait until Qui-Gon told him the details. Meanwhile, he had a crucial question burning on his lips, one that he did not dare ask: Did Qui-Gon know that today was his birthday?

Today he was thirteen. This birthday was an important occasion for a Jedi apprentice. He was now officially a Padawan. Traditionally, this birthday was not marked by a celebration, but observed quietly, with reflection and meditation. Obi-Wan was aware that as part of the tradition he would receive a meaningful gift from his Master.

Qui-Gon had not mentioned it this morning. Not as they ate, or prepared for the journey, or walked to the landing platform. Qui-Gon had barely spoken three words. Had he forgotten? Did he know? Obi-Wan was longing to remind Qui-Gon, but their relationship was too new. He wouldn't want his Master to think of him as greedy or self-important, or even worse, a nag.

Surely Yoda would have told Qui-Gon. Obi-Wan knew that the two Jedi Masters were in constant contact. Or perhaps the mission ahead was so important that Yoda had forgotten, too.

They skirted the last vendor, cut down an alleyway, and arrived at the landing platform. The Governor of Bandomeer had arranged a transport for them in gratitude for their work. She'd found a small trading vessel willing to take them on the journey to the planet of Gala. Obi-Wan knew that once they got on the ship, the talk would center on the mission ahead. Should he tell Qui-Gon it was his birthday now?

Ahead, a tall, gangly pilot loaded transport boxes onto his ship. Obi-Wan recognized the long, flexible arms of the Phindar. Obi-Wan quickened his pace to reach him, but Qui-Gon put a hand on his shoulder.

"Close your eyes, Obi-Wan," he instructed.

Obi-Wan groaned inwardly. *Not now!* he begged. He knew that Qui-Gon was about to drill him on a classic Jedi exercise: Attention to the Moment Gives Knowledge. At the Temple, Obi-Wan had always done well with the exercise. But he'd been distracted this morning, and could barely remember anything except his own birthday.

"What do you see?" Qui-Gon asked.

Eyes closed, Obi-Wan gathered his thoughts as though they had been feathers in a windstorm. He plucked observations out of the air, remembering things his eyes had registered but his mind had not.

"Small transport ship with one deep scratch in right flank, several dents on underside of cockpit. Phindian pilot with flight cap, goggles, and dirty fingernails. Twelve cargo boxes ready to be loaded, one flight bag, one medpac . . ."

"The hangar," Qui-Gon prompted gently.

"Old stone overhang with three docking bays. Cracks running vertically down the stone, a green vine trying to grow three meters down from the ceiling on the left, with one purple flower four meters down —"

"Six meters," Qui-Gon corrected sternly. "Open your eyes, Obi-Wan."

His eyes flew open. Qui-Gon's piercing blue gaze studied him, making him feel, as always, as though his lightsaber was dragging on the ground, or his tunic was stained.

"Are you distracted by something, Obi-Wan?" Qui-Gon asked.

"My first official mission, Master," Obi-Wan said. "I want to do well."

"You will do what you will do," Qui-Gon responded neutrally. He waited, his eyes never leaving Obi-Wan's face. It was forbidden for an apprentice to lie to a Master, to conceal the truth, or even shade it.

Obi-Wan willed his feet not to shift and his eyes to remain steady on Qui-Gon's. "Perhaps

I'm distracted by something more personal, Master."

A gleam of amusement suddenly lit Qui-Gon's eyes. "Ah. A birthday, perhaps?"

Obi-Wan nodded, a grin escaping.

"You would be expecting your gift, then." Qui-Gon frowned. He had forgotten, after all! But after only a moment, he reached into the pocket of his tunic. His large, strong hand emerged, concealing something hidden in his palm.

Obi-Wan stared expectantly. Masters usually thought for weeks or months about their gifts, often traveling to far reaches for a healing crystal, or a blanket or cloak from the weavers of the planet Pasmin, who wove garments of great warmth out of material so fine it was almost weightless.

Qui-Gon pressed a smooth, round stone into Obi-Wan's hand.

"I found it years ago," Qui-Gon explained. "When I was no older than you are now."

Politely, Obi-Wan stared at the stone. Did it contain some sort of power?

"I found it in the River of Light on my home planet," Qui-Gon continued.

And? Obi-Wan wondered. But Qui-Gon was silent. Obi-Wan realized that the present his

Master had given him was exactly what it appeared to be: a rock.

Qui-Gon was no ordinary Master. Obi-Wan knew that. So he looked at the present again. His fingers closed around the stone. It felt smooth and polished. He liked the way it felt in his hand. And when the sunlight hit it, he could see deep red streaks running through the shiny blackness. It was beautiful, he realized.

He met Qui-Gon's eyes. "Thank you, Master. I will treasure it."

"And did you complete the Padawan birthday ritual?" Qui-Gon asked. "Only by remembering the past are we able to learn from the present."

On his or her thirteenth birthday, each Padawan must take a quiet time for reflection. Both good and bad memories must be consulted and meditated on.

"I have not had time, Master," Obi-Wan admitted. His mission on Bandomeer had been full of dangers — he had been kidnapped and marooned on a mining platform, among other things. Qui-Gon knew he had not had time. Why was he asking?

"Yes, time is elusive," Qui-Gon said, unmoved. "But it is best to track it down. Come, the pilot is waiting."

Obi-Wan trailed after Qui-Gon, fighting off a feeling of hopelessness. Would he ever please his new Master? Just when he felt Qui-Gon had given him the strong base of his trust, he found himself hanging free. Now he realized that the only thing Qui-Gon had ever truly given him was a rock.

"Two minutes," the pilot called out to them as they approached. "I finish loading."

"I am Qui-Gon Jinn and this is Obi-Wan Kenobi," Qui-Gon introduced them.

"Yes, big surprise, Jedi are not hard to spot," the pilot mumbled, picking up a loading carton.

"And you are . . ." Qui-Gon waited.

"Pilot. I am what I do." He had the red-streaked yellow eyes of a Phindian, as well as hands that dangled near his ankles.

"You're a Phindian," Obi-Wan said. "I have a friend . . . someone I know is a Phindian. His name is Guerra." Guerra had been a fellow mining slave on the platform where Obi-Wan had been held captive. He had almost lost his life in order to save Obi-Wan.

"So I know him?" Pilot answered gruffly. "I am expected to know every Phindian in the galaxy?"

"No, of course not," Obi-Wan said, confused. The pilot's rudeness surprised him. It was almost as though Obi-Wan had offended him in some way.

"Then let me load, and you board," Pilot answered brusquely.

"Come, Obi-Wan," Qui-Gon directed.

Obi-Wan trailed after Qui-Gon into the cockpit, where they took their seats.

"For our first mission together, Yoda has chosen something he thinks will be routine," Qui-Gon told him. "Of course, Yoda also says, 'If routine you count on, disappointed your hopes will be.'"

Obi-Wan grinned. "It is better to expect nothing, and let each moment surprise you," he said. It is something he had been taught at the Temple.

Qui-Gon nodded. "The planet of Gala has been ruled for many years by the Beju-Tallah dynasty. They were successful in uniting a world with deep tribal hatreds. There are three tribes on Gala — the city people, the hill people, and the sea people. Over the years the Tallah rulers grew corrupt. They plundered the planet of wealth, and the people are close to revolt. The old Queen knows this. Instead of giving the throne to her son, Prince Beju, she has agreed to elections. The people will choose among three candidates. The Prince is among them. He has lived in seclusion for much of his life. The Queen feared for his safety. Yet he was trained as a ruler, and is anxious to gain the throne."

"Elections sound wise for the planet," Obi-Wan remarked.

"Yes, it is always wiser to adapt to change," Qui-Gon agreed. "Still, some continue to resist. Prince Beju, for example. We are told that he is not happy that he has to submit to a vote by the people. He considers the rule of Gala to be his birthright. We will be there as guardians of the peace, to make sure the elections go smoothly."

"Is there any sign that the Prince is planning something?" Obi-Wan asked.

"Yoda says not," Qui-Gon answered. "But he also said that we should not rely on that." Qui-Gon sighed. "It was a typical conversation with Yoda. So we should be prepared for anything."

Pilot climbed into the cockpit and sat down in the seat. He leaned over to set a course into the navi-computer. "I'll drop you on Gala and go on," he said. "Now sit tight and don't talk much."

Qui-Gon and Obi-Wan exchanged an amused glance. Were they being transported by the rudest pilot in the galaxy?

The ship took off, and within moments Bandomeer was just another planet, a grayish world in deep blue space. Obi-Wan stared out the viewscreen at it. Below him, friends he had made would go on with their lives.

"I wonder what Si Treemba is doing," he said softly.

"Putting his nose in places where it doesn't belong, most likely," Qui-Gon said. But Obi-Wan knew that the Jedi was just as fond of Si Treemba as he was. His Arconan friend had been loyal and brave.

"He and Clat'Ha will have their hands full on Bandomeer," Qui-Gon remarked, naming another friend. "The planet has a long way to go to reclaim their natural resources."

"I'll miss Guerra, too," Obi-Wan said with a sigh. "He was a loyal friend."

"Loyal?" Qui-Gon frowned. "He betrayed you to the guards. You almost died because of Guerra."

"But he saved me in the end," Obi-Wan reminded him. "Sure, the guards threw me off the mining tower. But Guerra made sure there was a sling for me to fall into."

"You were lucky, Obi-Wan," Qui-Gon said. "The Force helped you to land safely. No, I can't agree with you about your friend. If someone claims that he is not to be trusted, it is generally a good idea to take note of it. I'm not saying that

Guerra is bad, but I'd certainly be wary of such a character."

Suddenly, the ship veered and dipped alarmingly.

"Oops, sorry, very strange space shear," Pilot said. "Too much distracting talk behind me. Time for hyperspace."

The ship shot into hyperspace. Bandomeer disappeared in a rush of stars. Obi-Wan felt a thrill of excitement. He was off on his first official mission.

They were halfway to Gala when a warning light began to blink and beep insistently on the control panel.

"Don't worry," Pilot said. "Just a small fuel leak."

"Fuel leak?" Qui-Gon asked. The beeping suddenly shifted to a loud siren.

"Oops, worry," Pilot said. He shut off the indicator. "I must exit hyperspace and land on the nearest planet to our location." Swiftly, he entered information into the navi-computer. "Not a problem," he continued, whistling through his teeth.

The ship shuddered as it reentered normal space. Immediately, the comm unit came alive.

"Identify yourself!" a loud voice demanded.

"Ah," Pilot muttered. "This world is unfriendly."

"What planet is it?" Qui-Gon asked.

"Closed to outside ships," Pilot muttered.

"Identify or be destroyed!" the voice thundered.

"So find another planet!" Qui-Gon suggested sharply, beginning to lose his patience.

"Emergency." Pilot leaned into the comm unit. "We have emergency on board. And Jedi! It is a Jedi emergency! Asking permission to land —"

"Permission not granted! Repeat: permission not granted!"

Qui-Gon peered through the viewscreen. "Where are we, Pilot? We must be close to Gala. This should be a populated system. There has to be somewhere else to land!"

"Not so!" Pilot cried as he maneuvered the ship with a lurch to the right.

Not so? Obi-Wan heard the expression with a start. His friend Guerra had used it so many times!

"Why not?" Qui-Gon demanded.

Suddenly two starfighters appeared and split off with each other in order to flank them. Laser cannons began to fire.

"Because we're under attack!" Pilot screamed.

CHAPTER 3

Pilot began to take evasive action as the starfighters screamed toward them. Obi-Wan was thrown against the console.

"I think I can lose them!" Pilot shouted as the ship was rocked by laser fire.

"Stop!" Qui-Gon roared. He threw himself forward and wrenched the controls from Pilot's grasp. "Are you a fool? This transport can't out-maneuver two starfighters!"

"I'm a good pilot!" Pilot said wildly. "And can't you use that Force of yours?"

Qui-Gon gave him a sharp look, then shook his head. "We can't work a miracle," he said firmly. "The starfighters are escorting us down. If you don't follow them, they'll blast us right out of space."

Grudgingly, Pilot took the controls again. The starfighters wheeled and flanked them, guiding them down toward the planet's surface. When the landing platform was in view, they waited until they were sure that the transport ship was landing, then zoomed off.

Slowly, Pilot set the transport down. Qui-Gon strode to the viewscreens to get a full view of the landing platform. "Assassin droids are surrounding the ship," he reported.

"That doesn't sound good," Pilot said nervously. "I have a couple of blasters and a proton grenade —"

"No," Qui-Gon interrupted. "We will not fight. They're here to guard us until someone arrives. They won't attack us."

"I wouldn't be so sure," Pilot remarked, eyeing them.

"I'm ready, Master," Obi-Wan said.

"Then come." Qui-Gon activated the release lever for the exit ramp. He strode out, followed closely by Obi-Wan. Pilot lurked in the doorway.

The assassin droids turned toward them but their built-in blasters did not fire. "You see, they're here as escorts," Qui-Gon said quietly. "Don't make any sudden movements."

Obi-Wan walked down the ramp, keeping his eyes on the droids. They were killing machines, designed and programmed for battle without conscience or consequence. What kind of world had they landed on?

When they hit the bottom of the ramp, Qui-

Gon slowly raised his hands. "We are Jedi —" he began, but his words were cut off by blaster fire. The assassin droids were attacking!

Obi-Wan heard the flap of his Master's cape as Qui-Gon jumped and twisted, landing on a pile of old metal crates nearby. And Obi-Wan was moving too, moving before thought, leaping over the heads of the first line of droids. His lightsaber was already in his hand. He activated it and saw the reassuring blue glow.

He could hear the *click* and *whirr* of the droids' joints as they swiveled, trying to get better aim. The Jedi had the advantage of speed and better maneuverability. Obi-Wan found that, using the Force and his own perceptions, he could predict which way a droid would move.

Qui-Gon leaped down from the crate. With one stroke he sliced through three droids. Their metallic heads clattered to the floor and rolled. Their bodies twitched, puzzled, then collapsed.

Obi-Wan cut through the first droid on his right, then used his momentum to twist and roll into the legs of the second. The droid wobbled, trying to aim as Obi-Wan sliced through its spindly legs with his lightsaber. As soon as the droid fell, Obi-Wan dealt a blow to the control panel on its chest. The droid collapsed, inoperative.

But Obi-Wan was already moving on to the next, and the next. He could sense Qui-Gon's movements behind him, and knew that Qui-Gon was driving the droids back toward the crumbling wall of the landing platform. Fighting, slicing, always moving, Obi-Wan was able to reach the outer flank of the droids, allowing him to drive them back to where Qui-Gon wanted them.

There were only four droids left standing when the Jedi were able to maneuver them against the wall. Working in tandem, Qui-Gon and Obi-Wan avoided the constant blaster fire and, with a sudden movement, rushed the droids, slicing through their jointed legs. The four collapsed in a heap, and Qui-Gon attacked again, making sure they were down for good.

He turned to look at Obi-Wan. His blue eyes gleamed.

"So they weren't escorts," he said. "I was wrong. It happens."

Obi-Wan wiped the sweat off his face with the sleeve of his tunic. He returned his lightsaber to his belt.

"I'll remember that," he said with a grin.

Qui-Gon twisted, searching the hangar with a frown. "Where's that blasted Pilot?"

The Phindian was gone.

Qui-Gon strode back up the ramp into the ship. The control console had been disabled, hit by blaster fire.

"They must have ordered a droid to do that while the rest were fighting," Qui-Gon said with a frown. "Now we can't take off again."

Qui-Gon reached for his comlink. He pressed the coordinates to reach Yoda, but nothing happened. "Communications must be jammed on this world," he murmured. "Obviously, they don't want interference."

"What should we do, Master?" Obi-Wan asked.

"We need to talk to Pilot," Qui-Gon answered.

"But how will we find him?"

Qui-Gon's mouth tightened. "Don't worry. He'll find us."

CHAPTER 4

They left the landing platform and followed a narrow, twisting street into the heart of the city. Qui-Gon directed Obi-Wan to raise his hood to cover his face.

"We must be on Phindar," Qui-Gon murmured. "All those we've passed have been Phindians, and I know we're close to Gala. This is probably Laressa, their capital city. I do not think there are many alien people on this world. We must try not to attract attention. Keep your arms inside your cloak."

Obi-Wan obeyed him. "But Master, why do you say that Pilot will find us? How do you know?"

"Landing here was no accident, Obi-Wan."

It seemed like a complete accident to Obi-Wan, but he knew better than to say so. Instead he turned his attention to his surroundings. He was not distracted now. He forgot it was his birthday, forgot everything but watching how his Master moved through the streets. As they grew closer to the center of the city and the streets grew more crowded, Qui-Gon changed. Usually, the Jedi Master's bearing alone commanded attention. He was a large, powerfully built man and he moved with grace.

But on this planet, Qui-Gon moved differently. He lost what made him unique and shuffled along with the crowd. Obi-Wan watched, and learned. He, too, matched his pace to those around him. He glanced at what they glanced at, looked away, kept his eyes ahead, all with the rhythm of the passersby. He saw that Qui-Gon was doing the same. The look of fierce attention was gone from Qui-Gon's gaze, but Obi-Wan knew he was taking in everything.

Phindar was a strange world. The people were dressed simply, and Obi-Wan could see that their clothes had been mended many times. Readout signs in the shops announced in scrolling type NOTHING TODAY or CLOSED UNTIL SHIPMENT. Phindians would glance at the signs, sigh, and plod on further, their market baskets empty. Lines formed outside shuttered shops, as if the Phindians were willing to chance that they would open soon.

Assassin droids were everywhere, their joints clicking, heads rotating. On the muddy, unpaved street, gleaming silver landspeeders zoomed by with no regard for traffic rules or pedestrians attempting to cross.

A current ran between the people, and Obi-Wan reached out with the Force to meet and understand it. What was the feeling?

"Fear," Qui-Gon remarked quietly. "It's everywhere."

A group of three Phindians dressed in full-length metallic silver coats suddenly appeared on the walkway. They strode, shoulder to shoulder, their dark visors swallowing up the sunlight. The other Phindians quickly moved off the walkway into the muddy road. Obi-Wan's steps faltered, astonished. The people had moved so quickly and without thought, stepping into the mud with a reaction born of habit. The silver-coated Phindians didn't falter, but took charge of the walkway as if it were their right.

Qui-Gon gave Obi-Wan a hard tug on his cape, and quickly they both stepped off the paved walkway into the muddy street. The silver-coated men marched by.

As soon as they passed, the other Phindians, without a word, climbed back onto the paved walkway. Once again, they began the process of looking into shops, then turning away when they saw there was nothing for sale.

"Do you notice anything strange about some of them?" Qui-Gon murmured. "Look at their faces."

Obi-Wan gazed into the faces of the passersby. He saw resignation, desperation. But slowly he realized that on some faces he saw . . . nothing. There was a strange blankness in their eyes.

"Something is not right here," Qui-Gon remarked softly. "It is more than fear."

Suddenly, a large gold landspeeder screamed around a corner. The Phindians in the street scurried to safety, and the others on the walkway shrank back against the buildings.

Obi-Wan felt the dark side of the Force shimmer outward from the gold speeder. With a slight touch to his shoulder, Qui-Gon led Obi-Wan to withdraw silently and quickly. They faded back into an alley and watched the speeder blast by.

A silver-coated driver was at the controls. In the back were two figures. They wore long coats of gold. The Phindian woman had lovely orange eyes shot through with gold the color of her coat. The male next to her was larger than most, with the long, powerful arms of the Phindian people. He did not wear a mirrored visor, and his small, bronze-colored eyes swept the street arrogantly.

Obi-Wan didn't need a Temple lesson in order to pay attention. His senses were on alert. Qui-Gon was right. Something was very wrong. Every detail he had seen told him so. Evil was at work here.

The gold speeder zoomed around a corner, nearly hitting a child who was being frantically pulled along by her mother. Obi-Wan stared after the speeder, incredulous.

"Come, Obi-Wan," Qui-Gon said. "Let's go to the market."

They crossed the street into a large plaza. It was an open-air market like ones Obi-Wan had seen on Bandomeer and Coruscant. Only here, there were plenty of stalls, but nothing for sale. Some metal scraps, fit for nothing. A few rotten vegetables.

Still, the market was crowded with people milling about. Obi-Wan had no idea what they could be buying. In a shop window across the plaza, Obi-Wan saw a worker power up a read-out sign. The word flashed in red: BREAD. Suddenly, the mass of people began pushing and hurrying toward the shop. Within seconds, there was a line that snaked around the perimeter of the plaza.

Obi-Wan and Qui-Gon almost lost each other

in the confusion. Then, suddenly, a figure stood at Qui-Gon's elbow.

"So nice to see the Jedi again," Pilot remarked in a pleasant tone, as if he were admiring the weather. "Follow, please."

CHAPTER 5

Qui-Gon melted behind Pilot. Obi-Wan followed. He had no idea how Qui-Gon had known that Pilot would find them, or why Qui-Gon trusted him to lead them.

Pilot loped through twisting alleys and narrow side streets. He moved quickly, often looking from right to left, or up above to the rooftops, as if he were afraid they were being followed. Obi-Wan was sure that they doubled back on their trail a few times. Finally, Pilot stopped before a small café with a window so streaked with dirt that Obi-Wan could not glimpse the interior.

Pilot opened the door and hurried them through. It took a moment for Obi-Wan's eyes to adjust. A few small halo-lamps were mounted on the wall, but they did little to chase away the gloom. A half-dozen empty tables were scattered around the space. A faded green curtain hung in a doorway.

Pilot pushed aside the curtain and led the Jedi down a hallway past a tiny, cluttered kitchen to a smaller room at the back. The room was empty except for one customer who sat, his back to the wall, in an alcove farthest from the door.

The customer stood and spread his long Phindian arms.

"Obawan!" he cried.

It was Obi-Wan's friend Guerra!

Guerra's orange eyes beamed at Obi-Wan. "You come at last, friend! How glad I am to see you, no lie!"

"I'm glad to see you, too, Guerra," Obi-Wan answered. "And surprised."

"It is a surprise, ha!" Guerra chortled. "But I had nothing to do with it. Not so, I lie! I think you met my brother, Paxxi Derida."

Pilot smiled at them. "It is my honor to have brought you here. Good journey, yes?"

Qui-Gon raised an eyebrow at Obi-Wan. The cheerful Derida brothers were acting as though the Jedi had accepted an invitation for a friendly visit. Instead, they'd been hijacked, fired on, then abandoned.

Qui-Gon walked farther into the room. "So Pilot deliberately dumped that fuel, didn't he."

"Please do call me Paxxi, Jedi-Gon," Paxxi said amiably. "Of course I dumped fuel. We did not expect you to say yes to a Phindian journey."

"Did you know this?" Obi-Wan asked Guerra.

"No, I was unaware," Guerra answered earnestly.

"Not so, you lie, brother!" Paxxi said, digging Guerra in the ribs.

"True, I lie, I do!" Guerra agreed. "I was on the ship, hidden in the cargo hold. After I escaped the mining platform, there were those who wanted to bring me back to work in the mines. But I longed for Phindar. So here I am!"

"But why did you hide?" Obi-Wan asked. "And since you are native Phindians, why didn't you just land?"

"Good question, very smart, Obawan," Guerra said earnestly. "First of all, there is a blockade. And second, criminals are especially not welcome, even if they're natives."

"You're a criminal?" Obi-Wan couldn't believe it.

"Oh, yes, but such a little one," Guerra said.

"Not so, brother! You have a price on your head!" Paxxi chortled. "As do I! Assassin droids are ordered to shoot on sight!"

"So, it is true, brother!" Guerra agreed. "You are right again, for the first time!"

"Who put a price on your head?" Qui-Gon asked. Obi-Wan could see that he was both irritated and amused by the Deridas. "And why?"

"The Syndicat," Guerra answered. His amiable face grew grave. "Vast criminal organization who has gained control of Phindar. Things are very bad here, Jedi. I'm sure you saw, even in the short time you were here. They started the blockade. No one can leave, no one can land. But we thought even the Syndicat wouldn't oppose two Jedi in trouble. They would let you land, refuel, and take off again. Then my brother and I could sneak out and stay on Phindar. Easy plan!" Guerra congratulated himself. "Very smart! Not so," he amended with a look at Qui-Gon. "It didn't so happen that way. . . ."

"No, it didn't," Obi-Wan spoke up. "First of all, we were attacked by assassin droids. Now we're stuck on Phindar with no way to get off."

"Ah, I've thought of this!" Guerra exclaimed. "True, it seems you are stuck. But even though the main spaceport is tightly controlled by the Syndicat, there are ways to get people off-planet, if you have enough money."

"But we're Jedi," Obi-Wan said impatiently. "We don't have much money. Maybe *you* should pay, since it's your fault that we're stranded."

"True, Obawan! We should pay! Did you hear this, Paxxi?" Guerra asked, amused. He and Paxxi held on to each other's shoulders and laughed loudly in each other's face.

When they stopped, Guerra wiped tears from his eyes. "Good joke, Obawan. Very funny. We have no money. But no worry, please. We have a way to *get* money. Much money. We can do this easily. Well, not so — we might need a little help from Jedi."

"Ah," Qui-Gon said lightly. He fixed his penetrating blue stare on Guerra. "Now we finally get to the truth. Why don't you tell us the real reason you brought us here . . . and why you want us to stay?"

CHAPTER 6

Guerra smiled at Qui-Gon. "Wait, my friend. You seem to say that we deceived you, yes? Me, deceive my friend Obawan? How could such a thing be?"

Qui-Gon waited.

"Oh, my, perhaps I did so," Guerra said. "But for such a good reason!"

"What's the reason, Guerra?" Obi-Wan asked. "And this time, tell the whole truth."

"I always tell the whole truth to Obawan," Guerra assured him. "Well, not so. But now, I will for you, Jedi men of honor. But where to begin?"

"Why don't you tell us why there is a death order on your head," Qui-Gon suggested. "That seems like a good place to start."

"True, it is so! Well, I suppose the Syndicat would call me a thief," Guerra said. "And others as well."

"Not a thief, brother!" Paxxi interrupted. "A freedom fighter who steals!"

"True, thank you, brother," Guerra said, bowing to Paxxi. "That is what I am. And my brother as well. You see, the Syndicat controls everything. Food and materials, med supplies, heat, everything Phindians need to survive. Naturally, in such a situation, one must find ways to buy and sell things the Syndicat does not control."

"A black market," Qui-Gon supplied.

"Yes, so, a black market, you could say," Guerra agreed, nodding. "We steal a little here, sell a little there. But all for the good of the people!"

"And your own profit," Qui-Gon added.

"Well, that too. Shall we suffer more than we are already?" Paxxi asked. "But the Syndicat doesn't like this. If we are to steal, we must steal for them. This, we refuse."

"Why should we give our talents to a gang of thieves?" Guerra asked, pounding the table. "Of course, we are thieves ourselves. But honest ones!"

"So, my brother!" Paxxi agreed. "And we are not murderers and dictators."

"So, my brother!" Guerra nodded. "That's why we must free our beloved planet from the grip of these monsters. The Syndicat leader is

Baftu. He is a gangster without a conscience. He enjoys seeing the people suffer!" Guerra's orange eyes were mournful. "And his assistant Terra is no better, I am sorry to say. For all her beauty, her heart is black and cold."

"They must be the Phindians we saw in the gold landspeeder," Obi-Wan said.

"They were in gold coats?" Paxxi asked. "Yes, they are the ones."

Guerra and Paxxi shared a sad look. They shook their heads, their cheerfulness gone.

"What about the people we saw on the street?" Qui-Gon asked. "The ones with the blank faces."

Paxxi and Guerra shared another mournful look. Guerra sighed.

"The renewed," he said softly. "So sad."

"So," Paxxi agreed.

"It is the method of ultimate control," Guerra explained. "You know the memory wipe?"

Obi-Wan nodded. "It's used to reprogram droids. It removes all traces of their memory and training so they can be reprogrammed."

Guerra nodded. "The Syndicat has developed a device to do this to Phindians who they consider enemies or agitators. They memory wipe the person, then drop them on another world, somewhere terrible. The person has no memory of who they are or what they can do. It is a game for the Syndicat. They bet on how long the person will survive. A probe droid follows them and sends back holo-pictures of what happens. Most do not survive."

Qui-Gon's face went very still. Obi-Wan had seen that look before, a look that spoke of how deeply Qui-Gon was outraged at injustice and sheer cruelty.

"And some are not sent off-planet," Paxxi said softly. "That is saddest of all, maybe. Phindar is full of rootless people who do not remember their families, their loved ones. Or the things they could once do. They are helpless. Now Phindar is full of those who pass their fathers, their wives, their children on the street and do not recognize them."

"So you see," Guerra said, "the Syndicat will stop at nothing. Which brings us to how you can help."

"If the wise Jedi would be so kind," Paxxi added.

"You saw the signs in the shops, the marketplace," Guerra went on. "The Syndicat controls all the shortages. It is a method of time control, just as renewal is mind control. The shortages are fake. If the people are waiting in line all day just to feed their families, they don't have time to revolt, you see. Do you ever get enough? Not so. Supplies are doled out carefully so that you have to wait in line the next day as well."

"The Syndicat has stored everything we need," Paxxi continued. "Food, med supplies, building supplies, everything. It is all hidden in warehouses. We know this."

"And some of it is held in giant storage rooms underneath their headquarters here in Laressa," Guerra said. "So you see our plan? If we can liberate the goods, we can show the people that the Syndicat has been depriving them of food and medical supplies. They will rise in revolt! All we need is your help. I saw the Jedi mind control on the mining platform. Obawan convinced the guards to let him into storage. You see, he can do the same here!"

"Stop," Qui-Gon said flatly. "First of all, Jedi Knights aren't thieves. Second, we have our own mission. We are not here to interfere in another planet's problems. And, just for argument's sake, how are the two of you planning to get all those goods out of the building without a fight? And why do you think this will break the back of such a powerful criminal organization? Surely the Syndicat has enormous sums at their disposal. Why would breaking into one storage area change anything?"

"Aha! Good, Jedi-Gon. So smart, just like Obawan!" Guerra said, nudging Qui-Gon with a friendly shoulder. "Let's discuss. First I must tell you that the storage area must have another entrance. How else would they sneak goods in and out? So all we have to do is get inside, find the other entrance, and so easy! We take everything out!"

"Not so easy," Qui-Gon said.

"But worth the risk, I think," Guerra insisted. "Another point I must make — along with food, medical supplies, and weapons, Paxxi and I know there's a vault, too. All the Syndicat treasury is there!"

"A vault," Qui-Gon repeated. "That implies high security."

"Yes, so!" Guerra agreed happily. "But Paxxi and I have the key!"

"How did you get a key?" Obi-Wan asked.

"Ha! He asks how!" Guerra said to Paxxi.

"Ha!" Paxxi agreed. "Long story!"

"We have a way to get in the building, too," Guerra said. "You see? Easy. So? You will go?"

"Let me get this straight," Qui-Gon interrupted in disbelief. "You want two Jedi to help two common thieves steal a treasure from a bunch of gangsters?"

Obi-Wan was silent. He agreed with Qui-Gon.

It was not a Jedi-style mission. Yoda would never approve. As much as he liked Guerra, he was glad that Qui-Gon had raised the objection.

"Yes, exactly!" Guerra said, still cheerful in the face of Qui-Gon's irritation.

"Wait, brother, we should explain further," Paxxi said. "We should assure the Jedi that we are far more interested in liberating our people than in stealing treasure."

"So, of course!" Guerra agreed. "Not that a little treasure wouldn't help —"

Guerra was interrupted by a commotion coming from the café. Quickly, Paxxi slipped out of the room to investigate. Within moments, he was back.

"So sorry," he announced. "I'm afraid it's time to go. Assassin droids searching for us all, I fear!"

CHAPTER 7

Qui-Gon sprang to his feet. He was not anxious to meet up again with those deadly killing machines. "Is there a back door?"

"Better than that, Jedi-Gon," Guerra answered. "Follow me, please."

Guerra moved to the fireplace. He pressed something Qui-Gon could not see. The wall shifted, and an opening was revealed.

They heard a crash from the café. "Time to hurry, I think," Guerra remarked pleasantly. "You first, Paxxi. Show the way to Obawan."

Paxxi slipped into the opening, and Obi-Wan and Qui-Gon followed. Guerra came last, shutting the opening behind him. The steps were stone with a depression in the center from the pressure of hundreds of years of footsteps. Paxxi moved quickly, Obi-Wan on his heels. At the top of the stairs he pushed through a grate and disappeared.

Qui-Gon climbed out and saw that he was on the roof, as he expected. The opening for the secret staircase was concealed as part of the venting system. Guerra slid the grate back into place.

Qui-Gon moved close to the edge of the roof and dropped to his knees. He lay flat, then moved forward a few inches to peer over the side.

Assassin droids patrolled the streets below with jerky movements. Silver-coated Syndicat guards directed them, waving blasters. Swarms of the droids entered one shop or business after another. They threw chairs, tables, shelving, personal items out into the street as they moved. It was like a tribe of insects, picking each area clean. Any Phindians who had the misfortune to find themselves on the street quickly scurried away before the assassin droids or the Syndicat guards could adminster a blow with the butt of a blaster or a jolt from a force pike.

"It doesn't look like they're searching," Qui-Gon said in a low tone to Guerra, who had lay flat beside him. "It looks as though they mean to spread terror."

"Yes, so, Jedi-Gon!" Guerra agreed nervously. "And their plan is working."

Qui-Gon froze. "Footsteps," he said in Guerra's ear. "Coming up an outside staircase."

"Time to go," Guerra said. He pushed himself back out of sight.

They gestured to Obi-Wan and Paxxi to keep quiet. Using their long, powerful arms, the brothers swung themselves over to the next roof. Qui-Gon looked at Obi-Wan. The gap between the two roofs was wide. If Obi-Wan couldn't make the jump alone, Qui-Gon would have to carry him on his back.

He asked the question silently: Can you make it? Obi-Wan nodded instantly. Once again, Qui-Gon was impressed by his Padawan's sharp instincts. Obi-Wan always seemed to know what he needed from him.

The boy hesitated only a fraction of a moment. Qui-Gon saw him gather the Force around him. Then he ran with quick, long steps up to the roof's edge and jumped. The Force and Obi-Wan's own strength propelled him safely to the other side.

Qui-Gon leaped after him. Obi-Wan's courage often impressed him, as did his instincts.

The Derida brothers were already halfway across the second roof, using their long arms to push off from the ground, increasing their speed. Guerra glanced back to make sure the Jedi were following.

Qui-Gon and Obi-Wan caught up, and the four jumped to the next roof. There was a structure on top of this roof, a small power shed. They darted behind it. The four stood for a moment, listening, hoping their pursuer hadn't followed this far.

But they heard something leap onto the roof. Their pursuer was out of their line of sight, but gaining. Paxxi let out a soft groan. They moved quietly and quickly to the end of the roof. Guerra reached it first. He grabbed the edge of the roof and coiled his fingers around it, ready to leap.

Suddenly a hand reached out and grabbed him by the neck. Guerra made a strangling noise. Qui-Gon whirled, ready to strike at the Phindian female who held Guerra.

"Guerra, it's me! Kaadi!" the female said.

"K-K-aaa —" Guerra answered.

"Oh. So sorry." She dropped her hand from around Guerra's neck. "Just trying to stop you. You run so fast!"

"Not fast enough, I see!" Paxxi said joyfully. "Lucky for us! We have missed you, Kaadi."

Guerra, Paxxi, and Kaadi entwined their long arms around each other in a Phindian hug, squeezing three times to show their great affection. They pushed their faces close to each other and beamed smiles for a long moment.

Rubbing his neck, Guerra turned to the Jedi.

"Good friends to us Jedi-Gon and Obawan, meet Kaadi, good friend also."

"Qui-Gon and Obi-Wan," Qui-Gon corrected.

"That is what I say," Guerra agreed. "Kaadi's father owns the café where we almost got captured. It has long been a meeting place for rebels. She fights the Syndicat, too."

Kaadi grinned. She was a small female, with jet-black hair and yellow eyes shot with green. "I move goods. Do you need a spare part for a speeder? An energy battery?"

"No, thank you," Qui-Gon said politely. He seemed to be constantly surrounded by thieves on this planet.

"And any word of your good father Nuuta?" Paxxi asked sympathetically, ducking his head so that he could look at her directly.

Kaadi's smile faded, and she shook her head. "We will hear if he is no more, we think. News will reach us."

Guerra and Paxxi were silent for a moment. Both of them reached out and wrapped one long arm around Kaadi's slender frame.

"Her father is one of the renewed," Guerra explained to Qui-Gon and Obi-Wan. "He was sent to Alba."

Qui-Gon nodded sympathetically. Alba was a world in the midst of a bloody, chaotic civil war.

She gazed at him with her clear yellow-green eyes. "Yes, it is bad there. But to be Phindian is to hope."

"Yes," Qui-Gon said quietly. "You must always hope."

"But let me talk of why I chased you," Kaadi said. "I must tell the Derida brothers that you have been spotted. The Syndicat knows you have returned. Efforts have been redoubled to capture you."

"We are not afraid," Guerra said. "Not so, I lie!"

"Do you mean all that activity down there had to do with Guerra and Paxxi?" Qui-Gon asked.

Kaadi shook her head. "Not only. They are looking for the Jedi, too. But also, anyone they know to be a rebel. Terra and Baftu are beginning mass arrests. An important visitor is arriving, and they want to be sure there is no trouble. They are proclaiming that any acts of sabotage or disruption will be met with death or renewal. Even if you are *suspected* of such things."

"Who is arriving?" Qui-Gon asked curiously.

"Prince Beju from the planet Gala," Kaadi answered.

Qui-Gon and Obi-Wan glanced at each other.

"Our spies tell us that an alliance is planned," Kaadi said thoughtfully. "The Syndicat will fund the Prince's mission to retake the governing of his planet. The Prince has already created a false shortage of bacta on his planet."

"That's an awful thing to do," Obi-Wan said.

Qui-Gon had to agree — bacta was a medical miracle, healing even the most serious of wounds. "The injured on Gala will suffer needlessly," he observed.

"Yes, the Prince has no conscience, just like Baftu and Terra," Kaadi said. She pressed Guerra's hand for a moment. "I am sorry to say this. Now the Prince will return to Gala with the bacta from Phindar. He will be a hero to his people. Then the Syndicat will move in. They will control Gala as they control Phindar. It is planned so."

"And then they will take over the star system, one planet at a time, yes?" Guerra said softly. "Using fake shortages of what the people need. Wiping their memories. Assassin droids will kill opposition and others will be renewed." He blinked at Qui-Gon. "We have seen how quickly this method can work."

It was a cold-blooded plan. Qui-Gon knew that Guerra was most likely right when he said Gala would only be the first step.

He had tried to keep his distance from Paxxi and Guerra's schemes. But now he saw that there was more at stake than he'd thought. If they could destroy the Syndicat's grip on Phindar, his mission on Gala would be easier. He and Obi-Wan had to ensure that free elections would take place.

But there was more. Qui-Gon felt a deep stirring of anger. Kaadi's bravery in the face of her distress about her father had touched him. Even Guerra and Paxxi had moved him. Behind their clownish behavior was deep suffering. He could feel it. The living Force pulsed in the brothers, strong and pure. He didn't know if he could trust them completely, but he knew they deserved his help.

Sometimes, Qui-Gon reminded himself, *fate finds you.*

"We'll help you," Qui-Gon said to Paxxi and Guerra. Before the brothers could speak, he held up a hand to stop them. "But you must promise me something."

"Anything, Jedi-Gon," Guerra vowed.

"You will tell me the complete truth always," Qui-Gon ordered them sternly. "You will not withhold information, or shade it, or twist it. You will obey the Jedi rule to tell the clear, solid truth."

"Yes so, Jedi-Gon!" Guerra rushed to assure him while Paxxi nodded energetically. "For a hundred moons I would not lie to you again!"

"Never mind the hundred moons," Qui-Gon said. "Just do as I say."

Obi-Wan shot his Master a questioning glance. Qui-Gon could see that the boy didn't understand this decision. His interpretation of the rules was too strict. But he would follow his Master nonetheless.

"It is better to act quickly," Guerra said. "We should break into Syndicat headquarters tonight."

Kaadi looked pale. "Break into headquarters when you have a price on your head? Who thought of that?"

"I did," Guerra and Paxxi said together.

"Very brave plan, so?" Paxxi asked her.

"Maybe brave," Kaadi said. "Or maybe crazy."

"Brave or crazy, we shall see," Guerra said, unconcerned. "With Jedi along, what can go wrong?"

Qui-Gon gave the Derida brothers a look of rueful exasperation. "We'll find out tonight, I'm sure," he said.

CHAPTER 8

The Syndicat headquarters were housed in a once grand but now crumbling mansion with extensive security. There were heavy gates to get inside the compound, and a laser security beam over each door and window.

"All you have to do is get us by two guards," Guerra whispered to Qui-Gon. "We'll do the rest."

Qui-Gon hated having to rely on Guerra's honesty, but he had come too far now to turn back. He nodded.

Paxxi and Guerra led the Jedi around the compound to a back entrance. There, a guard in the usual long silver coat and dark visor stood, hand on a blaster slung in a holster crossed over his chest.

There was nothing to do but walk straight up to him. "Good evening," Qui-Gon said. "We have an appointment."

The guard's head tilted to take in the two Jedi and the two Phindians. They couldn't see his eyes. "Move along, worm."

Qui-Gon brought the Force to bear. He surrounded the Syndicat guard's mind with his own will. "Of course, we may enter," he said.

The guard lowered his blaster. "Of course, you may enter," he repeated.

"You see, my brother Paxxi!" Guerra exulted. "The Jedi are powerful. I do not lie!"

"I see, brother Guerra," Paxxi said. "It is so!"

They walked quickly through a small yard packed with silver landspeeders, speeder bikes, and a few gravsleds. Another guard stood before a wide stone staircase leading to the back door of the mansion.

He stepped forward, raising his blaster. "Who are you and what is your mission here?" he challenged.

Again, Qui-Gon summoned the Force. With guards like these, it was easy to overpower their small minds. They were used to taking orders and rarely thought independently.

"We are welcome to look around," Qui-Gon said.

"You're welcome to look around," the guard said blankly, lowering his blaster.

They walked past him and up the stairs.

Beams of laser security crisscrossed the doorway.

"Your turn," Qui-Gon said to Guerra.

"Ah, I do nothing," Guerra said. "You'll see."

A second later, the beams shut off. The door opened. An older Phindian woman with dark hair threaded with silver stood facing them. She wore the long silver coat of the Syndicat guards. Qui-Gon tensed, but she waved them inside.

"Quickly," she said.

They stepped into a grand room with gilded walls of brilliant green stone. Soft rich carpeting was under their feet, covering the floor. The windows were hung with shimmering tapestries.

"All looted from our citizens," Guerra murmured.

The woman led them down a hallway. It must have been built for droids or servants, for it was narrow and the floor was a dull gray stone. A long bin with various pegs and shelves held a number of weapons — blasters, force pikes, and vibro-shivs.

"For the guards to take as they go out into the streets," Paxxi explained. "They are always well armed."

"Yes so, just more weapons to shoot us with!" Guerra said cheerfully.

The older woman led them to a narrow door. "Here. No security on downstairs now, but you must hurry. Now I must go," she said. Before any of them could thank her, she left, hurrying down the hall.

"She enjoys her work," Guerra said, watching her disappear. "She can't wait to return. Not so, I lie," he said softly. "The silver coat she wears has a tracking device in the fabric. She is monitored all the time. If Duenna spends too much time in the wrong place, assassin droids will track her down and ask her politely to return to her post. Not so, I lie! They kill her on the spot."

Paxxi opened the door. A stone staircase led downward. Paxxi started along the way, and they followed.

The staircase took them to a large empty room.

"First storage space," Paxxi said. "Empty, my brother. Strange, or not so?"

"It is so," Guerra said. He walked through a doorway into another space. It was also empty. Hurrying now, Guerra and Paxxi passed from room to empty room in the vast storage level.

"All gone," Paxxi said.

"Yes so," Guerra agreed sadly.

"You risked our lives for this?" Obi-Wan asked, incredulous.

Qui-Gon was just as irritated as Obi-Wan, but he tried to keep calm. "Didn't you check your information? Or did your spy betray you?"

"Not so, Jedi-Gon!" Guerra cried, flustered. "Duenna is on our side!"

"How can you be so sure?" Qui-Gon asked. "Never mind. We have to get out of here."

Suddenly they heard a slight whirring noise. Qui-Gon cocked his head. He knew that noise. But something about it was strange. He did not expect to hear it indoors.

"Speeders," Obi-Wan said.

A small floater suddenly zoomed around a corner, driven by a Syndicat guard. Behind him appeared three more floaters. Guards drove the speeders, and each had an assassin droid behind him. The first guard maneuvered his speeder to get a clear shot at Paxxi.

"Move!" Qui-Gon shouted. He reached out with the Force and propelled Paxxi backward. The blaster fire missed him by inches as he slammed against the wall.

Obi-Wan's lightsaber was in his hand in a movement so fast it was just a blur of pulsating light. He slashed at the guard, but was only able to knock the hand off the droid behind him on the speeder. Qui-Gon leaped forward but the speeder zoomed ahead, almost knocking him down. Qui-Gon was only able to deliver a glancing blow to the guard.

Suddenly, a slender beam of red light shot out from the wall, straight at Guerra. Guerra saw it and began to move. Qui-Gon saw the light, too, and summoned the Force to help. Guerra leaped over the beam just in time.

"Disruptor beams!" Qui-Gon shouted to Obi-Wan. The weapon had been outlawed on most worlds. It sent a visible blast of energy capable of cutting someone in two.

Obi-Wan charged at a floater heading for him and struck the driver across the neck with his lightsaber. The driver cried out and lost control of the floater, which crashed into the wall, knocking him unconscious. A disruptor beam suddenly shot out from the wall and hit the assassin droid, whose right-hand controls suddenly smoked and sputtered. The droid fell, but began to push off with his left-side controls. Meanwhile, the beam came straight at Obi-Wan, who leaped over it, twisting in midair to land safely next to Qui-Gon.

"The beams are triggered by movement," Qui-Gon said tersely. "Others are on constantly. Avoid them at all costs. Use the Force, Padawan." Qui-Gon turned and sliced at the assassin droid from the downed floater, cutting off its head. Then he leaped forward and lunged at the next floater. He dealt a glancing blow to the guard as it zoomed past and leaped over a disruptor beam.

The beams left on were easy to avoid, if the Jedi didn't allow themselves to be maneuvered into them. It was harder to predict where the beams triggered by movement would strike. Qui-Gon reached out for the Force, drawing it around him, feeling it, gaining strength from it. He sent his sense out to meet Obi-Wan's so that the Force would multiply and fill the room.

A floater headed for Paxxi, who bounded away, using his arms to propel himself. Qui-Gon knew the brothers had no weapons. He leaped after the floater, avoiding a disruptor beam with a twist of his body. Obi-Wan was already moving to the left, and they flanked the floater in a pincer movement, driving toward it with their lightsabers slashing. The guard fell backward from the blows, knocking himself and the assassin droid off the floater. Blaster fire came at Qui-Gon from his right, but he was already twisting to the left. He half turned to deliver a final blow to the guard.

The guards on the two remaining floaters were more agile. They drove Qui-Gon and Obi-

Wan before them into the next room. Since the ceilings were high, the Syndicat drivers could easily avoid the disruptor beams by flying higher, then zooming down to assault Obi-Wan and Qui-Gon.

The drivers of the floaters drove them relentlessly. It became a game to them. They laughed as they aimed at the Jedi, sending them leaping out of the way.

Qui-Gon and Obi-Wan developed a strategy born of desperation: run, turn, fight, reverse, and run again. Disruptor beams sizzled around them. One hit Qui-Gon's lightsaber and the shock sent a jolt of pain up his arm.

The faceless guards were determined, the assassin droids keeping up a steady stream of blaster fire. So far, the armor protected the Syndicat guards well. Qui-Gon began to deflect blaster fire at any part of them exposed, neck, wrists, their booted feet. Obi-Wan did the same.

Qui-Gon could see that Obi-Wan was tiring. His own legs ached from the constant running and leaping to avoid the beams and blaster fire. They could not hold out for much longer. The guards drove them from room to room. Qui-Gon began to see that the rooms formed a kind of maze. He tried to keep his focus. He doubted that he remembered how to reach the exit. They had lost Paxxi and Guerra completely. He only hoped that the brothers had found a place to hide.

At last they reached a room where the disruptor beams were thicker than before. They crisscrossed the room in a thick web. It would be impossible for the Jedi to evade them.

The whirr of the two floaters was behind them now. Any moment they would burst into the room. Qui-Gon quickly took several steps back from the threshold of the room until he was almost in the corner. He directed Obi-Wan to take the opposite corner. Obi-Wan nodded gravely at Qui-Gon, letting him know that he had guessed the desperate plan Qui-Gon had devised.

They would have to gauge the exact speed and height of the floaters a second before they appeared. Then they would run, using their momentum and the power of the Force to leap into the air. They would attack the first speeder, colliding with it in midair, hoping to dislodge both the pilot and the droid. And then they would have to land safely themselves.

There was no time to review. Qui-Gon only hoped Obi-Wan could follow him.

The whirr of the floater grew closer. Qui-Gon began to charge. Obi-Wan took off at the same moment. They built up speed in the huge room as they ran, and both lifted off the ground at the exact moment the floater burst into the room.

Qui-Gon had time to see the surprised gape of the Syndicat guard before he hit him full in the chest. The guard flew off the bike, with Qui-Gon managing to get in a lightsaber blow to his neck as he fell. The assassin droid had time to fire a quick burst before Obi-Wan hit him, feet-first, and sent him flying.

The power of their leap kept them in midair. Obi-Wan somersaulted before landing.

Then the second floater burst into the room and immediately collided with the first. The crash sent the second guard and droid flying. The two floaters kept moving through the air and hit a disruptor beam, which sent them careening out of control. The room shook as they crashed into the wall.

Suddenly, a portion of the huge wall dislodged with a groan, revealing an opening. The disruptor beams sizzled and went silent.

The Syndicat guards were just as surprised as the Jedi. Only the assassin droids kept moving, damaged but not destroyed. One had lost an arm, one a piece of its control panel. Their blasters were still operational. The shots missed the Jedi by a distance so small it sounded like a whisper by their ears.

The Force told Obi-Wan and Qui-Gon to jump, and they did, vaulting over the guards to attack the assassin droids first. Qui-Gon cut through one, rendering it worthless. Obi-Wan went straight for the other's control panel and with a stab from his lightsaber turned it into a sizzling junk heap.

The Syndicat guards had recovered from the surprise of being knocked off their floaters and uncovering a hidden room. They pulled out force pikes and advanced on the Jedi.

Qui-Gon and Obi-Wan stood their ground, lightsabers held down, pointing to the floor. Qui-Gon counted off the seconds in his head. He hoped his Padawan would have the same battle rhythm. They would need to keep their heads clear, their blows methodical. They could not let their exhaustion drive them. He reached out to the Force. It surged around him now; he had only to tap into it.

The Syndicat guards were still a few steps away when Obi-Wan leaped forward. *Too early!* Qui-Gon cried in his head. But he sprang to the right to cover Obi-Wan's flank. Obi-Wan attacked in a fury, his lightsaber a blue blur in the dimness. Qui-Gon had to match his speed or be unable to protect him. He tried to slow down the boy's rhythm, but Obi-Wan had let his exhaustion push his control to the breaking point.

Qui-Gon realized that he could not always count on Obi-Wan to pick up on his pacing. Something to work on later, when they had time. If they had time.

Together the Jedi slashed and jabbed, always moving, ducking, rolling, lunging until they had defeated their opponents. The two Syndicat guards fell heavily.

Qui-Gon stepped over them, sheathing his lightsaber in the same movement. He went to the opening and peered inside.

"I think we found the vault," he told Obi-Wan.

CHAPTER 9

A voice came from behind them. "Good work, Jedis!" Guerra approved in a hushed, reverent tone.

"We knew that even though you were greatly outnumbered, you would win," Paxxi assured them.

Qui-Gon lifted an eyebrow. "Not so?"

"So!" the brothers chorused.

Obi-Wan tried to control his shallow breathing. The last stand against the guards had drained him of his energy. He knew that he had been at the edge of his control. Qui-Gon had remained cool and methodical, covering any sloppy moves of Obi-Wan's with his own swift strokes. Although they had defeated the guards, Obi-Wan was disappointed in himself. He knew he given in to his impatience and had lost his focus. It had been a difficult fight.

"Thanks for your help," Obi-Wan said irritably, deactivating his lightsaber.

"Oh, we help by hiding, Obawan," Guerra assured him. "The Derida brothers are no good in a battle. We'd be in the way."

"Yes, you are so much better at fighting!" Paxxi said, beaming.

Obi-Wan wiped the sweat from his forehead with his sleeve. He wished he could feel as enthusiastic as the Deridas about his abilities.

He turned to find Qui-Gon studying him. "You fought well, Padawan," his Master said quietly. "Next time, you will do better. It is time to focus on the now. We achieved our aim here."

"Yes, you found the vault! Excellent!" Guerra exclaimed. He frowned when he took in the fallen Syndicat guards and assassin droids. "This isn't good. We have to leave without the Syndicat knowing we were here. It is better so."

"I'll find a place to hide them," Paxxi said.

"Paxxi is good at that," Guerra said.

"We won't ask why," Qui-Gon said with a sigh.

"No, is better so," Guerra agreed. "But first, we should take the armor coats. Might come in handy. Blaster fire seems to follow Jedi."

"You're the one who brought us here!" Obi-

Wan cried. He couldn't help being irritated at Guerra. He was beginning to realize how his friend twisted facts to suit his own purposes.

"True, Obawan!" Guerra said cheerfully. "You make a point!"

Paxxi found an equipment room piled with old parts for speeders and various circuits. There was inch-thick dust on the parts and the floor.

"Good," Qui-Gon approved. "The room is no longer used. The guards won't be discovered for quite some time."

Using the floaters and carefully avoiding the remaining disruptor beams, they transported the fallen guards and droids there. They took four armor coats and visors with them and closed the panel door behind them.

"I saw a pen for the floaters by the stairs, so we can leave them there," Guerra said. "Now let's see the vault."

"Let us go first," Qui-Gon directed. "Obi-Wan and I will alert you to disruptor beams."

But before they could take a step, a comlink embedded in one of the coats began to signal.

"Guard check," a voice said. "Guard check. Why were disruptor beams activated?"

Guerra's orange eyes went wide. Paxxi threw a hand to cover his mouth. Qui-Gon frowned.

He found the comlink and activated it, using the Force to respond in a way that would not draw attention. "Routine check. Repeat, routine check. All safe below. Suggest shutting off disruptor security beams on lower level for further check."

"Done."

With a buzzing noise, the disruptor beams retracted.

"Beams retracted," Qui-Gon said.

"End shift," the voice responded. "Leave premises. Lockdown in ten minutes."

"Message received," Qui-Gon responded. He shut off the comlink and looked at the others. "We don't have much time."

"Then we must hurry," Paxxi said.

They hurried to the vault and eased into the wall opening. Obi-Wan gasped. He had thought the room upstairs was grand. This room glittered with treasures. Rich rugs were piled on the floor, one on top of the other. Sleeping platforms were draped with the finest, softest coverlets. Large pillows embroidered in golden and silver threads were stacked next to the platforms.

Qui-Gon prowled, looking at the various boxes

and cartons stacked along the wall. "There's enough food and medical supplies here to last for months."

"Music, hologram visuals," Paxxi said, poking into another corner.

"Emergency supplies and weapons," Obi-Wan added, checking the cartons near him.

"It's their sanctuary," Qui-Gon said. "They could last here for months if they had to."

"Here!" Guerra called.

They hurried toward him. A door with a control panel was almost completely concealed in the corner.

"This must be the treasury," Guerra said.

"Well, at least you were right about that," Qui-Gon said.

"All right, break in," Obi-Wan urged. "We don't have much time."

Guerra looked at Paxxi. Paxxi looked at Guerra.

"Of course, Obawan, no problem," Paxxi agreed. "Oops, I lie, not so! Just one problem."

Qui-Gon closed his eyes and took a breath, as if to gather his shredded patience. "What?"

They both looked at the floor. "Ah," Guerra said. "So. We told the whole truth, yes. But not the *complete* whole truth. Yes, we can break in to the treasury. So easy! But we need something first. You see, the Syndicat robbed *us* first. They broke into our hiding place and stole everything! Everything we had spent so much effort and time to accumulate —"

"To *steal*," Obi-Wan corrected.

"Just so, Obawan, we stole it, yes, but only to sell it back to the people," Guerra said earnestly. "We had speeder parts, circuits, engines — all the things we used to have here on Phindar in great abundance, but no more. We would sell to the people for much cheaper prices than the Syndicat! So you see we do a great public service —"

"Just stick to the facts, Guerra," Obi-Wan interrupted impatiently. His friend was really beginning to test their friendship. Why hadn't Guerra told them this before?

"Of course, good advice, Obawan," Paxxi agreed. "So they stole from us. But what they did not know is that among those things was something very valuable."

"Something my good brother Paxxi invented," Guerra added eagerly. "An anti-register. It can undo the action of a transfer register."

The two brothers nodded and smiled at the Jedi. A transfer register was a method of recording transactions in the galaxy. An electro-optical device recorded the prints of buyers and sellers.

"Paxxi's device can duplicate any print in a security or registration system," Guerra told them.

Obi-Wan understood at once. Paxxi's anti-register device could be valuable beyond measure. It would allow the user to seize property and goods and break into any print-reliant security system throughout the galaxy.

"That device is very dangerous," Qui-Gon said quietly.

"Dangerous?" Guerra asked. "Not so, Jedi-Gon! It will help us!"

"But if the Syndicat knew you had it — if *anyone* knew, it would put you in great danger."

Paxxi waved a hand. "We are not afraid. Not so! I lie, of course we are. But that makes us careful. We can steal the treasury, leave the planet if we have to, even sell the device on the black market —"

"Can you imagine how much it's worth?" Guerra chortled. "Twelve fortunes!"

Qui-Gon looked stern.

"Not that this is important," Guerra hurriedly said. "First, we break the Syndicat, yes?"

"Which brings us back to the problem, my brother," Paxxi said. "Our stolen goods were here. Now they're not. So," he said to Qui-Gon, "we can't break in."

"Yet," Guerra added. "But so, we will."

"As soon as we find the device," Paxxi added helpfully.

"We had better return," Guerra said. "Lockdown will be soon. Duenna will be waiting."

With an exasperated sigh, Qui-Gon followed them from the room. They located the device that moved the wall, and it slid smoothly back into place. Then they took the floaters back to the pen behind the staircase. Quickly, they headed up to the main level.

"You're late," Duenna whispered worriedly when they appeared. Her bright orange eyes swept the corridor behind her. Then her tense face softened when she looked at Paxxi and Guerra. "But I am glad to see you. They ordered a random routine sweep of the lower floors. I could not warn you."

"We took care of the guards," Paxxi assured her. "But downstairs is empty now. No goods are stored."

"So sorry to tell you now," Duenna said, walking quickly down the corridor with them. "I just found out after I left you. The supplies were moved to the warehouse by the spaceport. Most of them will be loaded onto Prince Beju's transport to be taken back to Gala." She paused near the door. "Now you must go. Quickly! Terra and Baftu have returned. Lockdown is in only a few minutes."

"Duenna!" The voice was sharp, commanding. Footsteps clicked in the corridor off to the right. "Duenna!"

Duenna's face went pale. "It is Terra!" she whispered.

CHAPTER 10

The corridor was wide and empty. There was nowhere to hide. Duenna put a finger to her lips. Then she scurried around the corner into the adjacent corridor.

Qui-Gon commanded them all with his sharp blue gaze to be still. He pondered their situation. Terra was only meters away. Obi-Wan's hand drifted to the hilt of his lightsaber, prepared for anything.

"No need to run me down, old woman." Terra's voice cracked like a whip. "Where have you been?"

"In the kitchens," Duenna said. Her voice was a murmur.

"In the kitchens. Eating again? Or avoiding me? Look at me."

There was a pause. Guerra and Paxxi suddenly reached out and gripped each other's shoulders.

Terra's voice slowed to a purr. "What are you hiding from me, Duenna? Have you seen Paxxi and Guerra?"

Paxxi and Guerra squeezed each other hard.

"Not so, I have not," Duenna replied. Her voice was steady.

"Yet you are not surprised to hear they are on Phindar," Terra said.

"I am surprised," Duenna said. "I choose not to show it."

"Insolent!" Terra's voice now shimmered with anger. "Perhaps I should warn you, old woman. If you see Paxxi or Guerra, if you even talk to those traitors, I will personally see to it that you are renewed!"

Paxxi and Guerra looked at each other with stricken expressions.

"But not before you see the brothers die before your eyes," Terra hissed.

"No!" Duenna cried. "I beg you —"

"Beg if you wish," Terra said. "Obviously, there isn't a level you won't sink to. You do my bidding, clean my clothes, pick up my trash, why should you not beg me?"

"I would beg, if you would only hear me," Duenna said in a shaky voice. "If only you would hear what you were, what you could be again —"

"Enough! Hear me, Duenna. Any contact with

them, they die. And your memory is gone forever, old woman. But don't worry — I will choose the most terrible planet I can to drop you on! Now come with me. I need my bath drawn."

Terra's forceful footsteps headed off. They heard Duenna's softer tread behind hers.

"Come," Guerra whispered. "We must go."

They slipped into the silver armor coats and mirrored visors. It was easy to mingle with the rest of the Syndicat guards as they left the building.

As soon as they reached the dark street, Guerra led them down a narrow alley. There, they removed the coats and visors. Guerra put them in the satchel he carried.

"Why does Terra suspect that Duenna will contact you?" Obi-Wan asked the Derida brothers. "Does she know that Duenna is a rebel sympathizer? Isn't it dangerous to use her?"

"Not so," Guerra said softly. "Terra knows nothing for sure. She is afraid Duenna will contact us because she knows Duenna is our mother."

Obi-Wan shot a surprised glance at Qui-Gon. "But why is she working for the Syndicat?"

Qui-Gon wanted to hear what the Phindian brothers had to say.

Guerra and Paxxi exchanged a rueful look.

Paxxi nodded at Guerra. "The Jedi should know," he said.

"Yes, so," Guerra said sadly. "Duenna works for Terra because Terra is her daughter."

"So Terra is —"

"Our sister," Paxxi said.

"She is not the sister we had," Guerra explained. "Not the one we knew. She was renewed when she was only eleven years old. The Syndicat raised her. She had no memory of the girl she used to be. She grew up here, in this place, with cruelty and power."

"With no love," Paxxi said gently.

"So this is why our mother sacrificed her life," Guerra said. "She thought even as a servant, she could give Terra love. Maybe bring back part of the girl she knew." Guerra shrugged. "Yet it was never so. Terra did not change. Duenna still remains. She will stay and watch over her daughter — no matter what she is. No matter what she has become."

CHAPTER 11

That night, Guerra and Paxxi shared their cramped quarters with Qui-Gon and Obi-Wan. It was a tiny room in the small house that Kaadi shared with her family. She had insisted the brothers stay with her once she'd found them, and she welcomed the Jedi just as warmly.

They bedded down for the night on blankets spread on the floor. Paxxi fell asleep immediately, and Qui-Gon was in the state the Jedi called restful-sleep-in-danger, his eyes closed but a corner of his mind alert at all times.

Obi-Wan could not sleep. He could not stop thinking about what it must be like to lose your memory. He could not imagine anything more terrible. He had worked so hard at the Temple, made deep friendships, learned so much from Yoda and the Masters. What if all that was taken away from him?

"Are you awake, Obawan?" Guerra whispered from the blanket next to him.

"Yes," Obi-Wan answered softly.

"Yes so, I thought so," Guerra said. "I heard you thinking. You are still angry with me?"

"I'm not angry with you, Guerra," Obi-Wan said. "Maybe I was impatient with you. You never tell the whole truth."

"Not so," Guerra whispered. "Oh, I lie. You are right, Obawan, as you are always. I sense that you do not agree with the decision of Jedi-Gon to help us."

"Not so," Obi-Wan said. ". . . Or so. Maybe I lie."

"Ah, you tease me," Guerra said mournfully. "And this I deserve from you, I know."

"Why didn't you tell me about your sister?" Obi-Wan asked.

"Terra," Guerra murmured. He let out a gusty sigh. "She is my enemy, is she not, and yours? Yet it was not always so. You must believe this. If you could have known her as a child! Sunny and bright and eager! And funny! She was our tagalong, we called her, my good brother Paxxi and I. Baftu took all that was good and erased it, then filled in the spaces with hate. You see why we must crush them, Obawan? That is why Duenna risks so much — she and Paxxi think if the Syndicat is no more, they can reach Terra again."

"Do you think so?" Obi-Wan asked.

Guerra sighed again. "No, friend," he said. "I do not. But I hope so. Just as my family does. In some cases, some strong-minded beings can resist the effects of the memory wipe. They can hold on to flashes of memory. Just scraps of things — a face, a smell. A feeling. I fear it is not so for Terra. It has been so long for her. I have not the belief that my good brother does. I have only this tiny hope in my heart."

"It's something to hold on to," Obi-Wan said.

"Yes so," Guerra said quietly. "So if I tricked my friend, if I maybe did not tell him everything in the beginning, maybe my good friend Obawan will understand and grant me his help again."

A pause stretched between them. Obi-Wan's irritation at Guerra left in a rush. He saw the terror and pain that Guerra had lived with. Just as on the mining platform, when Guerra had covered his fear of certain death with smiles and jokes, here on Phindar he would do the same. Qui-Gon had been right to help them. Obi-Wan knew that now.

"Of course I will help you," he whispered, but Guerra was already asleep.

                    *   *   *

The following night, Obi-Wan, Qui-Gon, Guerra, and Paxxi slipped the armor coats over their clothes and donned the visors. Under the shelter of an overhang, they watched the activity at the warehouses by the spaceport.

There didn't seem to be high security. Syndicat members entered and exited the buildings without showing passes. They would only have to pretend to be delivering a shipment for cover. Or at least they hoped so.

Paxxi and Guerra had worked all day to gather authentic-looking supplies. Although their containers were marked "Bacta" and "Medpacs," they were actually filled with old circuit parts. But at least they would have something to carry inside.

"As soon as we're inside, we should split up into two groups," Qui-Gon instructed. "Guerra, go with Obi-Wan, Paxxi with me. We'll start at opposite ends and meet in the middle, if we can. If you locate your goods and find the anti-register device, leave. If we can't find it, we all exit the building in twenty minutes. We can't take any chances."

"But what if we don't find it?" Paxxi asked.

"We try again," Qui-Gon said. "We can't risk being discovered. The sooner we get out of there, the better." He turned to Obi-Wan. "Don't forget to keep your hands in your pockets so that no one can tell how long your arms are. We must look like Phindians."

Obi-Wan nodded. The four walked quickly across the courtyard. At the door of the warehouse, Qui-Gon barked out, "Delivering bacta," to the guard at the door. The guard waved them through.

Inside was a vast, high-ceilinged space. Row after row of transparent shelving units went from one end of the building to the other. Each shelf was piled with bins and cartons. Syndicat members in silver armor coats loaded supplies onto floaters, then headed for the large loading dock in the rear.

Paxxi and Guerra stopped, their faces registering shock. Obi-Wan knew why. Here was row after row of everything the Phindian people desperately stood in line for. Med supplies. Food. Parts to make their speeders run, their droids and machines operational. All hoarded by the Syndicat. The brothers had known this, but seeing it all with their own eyes must have been like receiving a blow.

"Keep moving," Qui-Gon said in a pleasant tone that hummed with urgency underneath.

Hands in his pockets, Obi-Wan headed off

with Guerra to the far end of the warehouse. They quickly strode down row after row. Other Syndicat members sometimes passed them. They would nod and keep going.

"This is easy, Obawan!" Guerra whispered. "So glad we stole these coats!"

Suddenly, the comlink in Guerra's coat began to signal him.

"Guard K23M9, report in," a voice said. "Explain whereabouts."

"It's probably a routine check," Obi-Wan murmured.

Guerra activated the comlink. "Warehouse delivery," he said.

After a pause, the comlink crackled. "Unscheduled. Explain."

Guerra looked at Obi-Wan in a panic. "Tell him he's mistaken," Obi-Wan whispered.

"Not so!" Guerra said rapidly into the comlink. "Orders received." He shut off the comlink.

"We'd better do this fast," Obi-Wan muttered.

They turned down the next row. As Guerra scanned the shelves, Obi-Wan kept watch.

"Found it, Obawan!" Guerra cried softly. "There, top shelf! I recognize my carton of energy cells. It must be here." He climbed up on the bottom shelf, then reached up with his long arms. He grabbed a carton and hauled it down.

Peering inside, he smiled broadly. "It's here, at the bottom."

Obi-Wan shoved the carton marked "Bacta" in its place. "All right, let's go."

They strode down the aisle, trying to look as though they weren't hurrying. An announcement suddenly boomed out of a speaker near them.

"Guard K23M9, report to security. Guard K23M9, report to security."

"That's me! What should we do, Obawan?" Guerra asked, panicked.

Obi-Wan thought carefully. They had to get the anti-register device out of the building. "Give me your coat," he ordered Guerra.

Guerra hesitated. "But that will put you in danger, Obawan. This I did once on Bandomeer. But this I will not do again."

"The Force will protect me," Obi-Wan told him, even though he doubted it. "You must find Qui-Gon and get that device out of here."

"You can use your Force to escape?" Guerra asked.

"Yes. Hurry." Obi-Wan slipped out of his own coat. Reluctantly, Guerra did the same. They exchanged the armor coats. Guerra put on Obi-Wan's and tucked the carton containing the anti-register device under his arm.

"Now go," Obi-Wan told him as Syndicat guards suddenly appeared around the corner on floaters.

Guerra swiveled and walked away, past the guards who headed for Obi-Wan. They did not give him a glance. Obi-Wan turned and saw four more guards heading for him in the opposite direction. He knew he could not resist. Even if he were to get past the guards here, security would lock down the building, and Guerra would never make it out. There was only one thing he could do. He had to surrender.

Guerra disappeared around a corner. The guards sped up to him and hovered, their blasters pointed at his neck, the only unprotected part of him.

"Guard K23M9, you are out of your quadrant," one of them said. "You know the penalty. We will escort you to headquarters. Resist, and you're dead."

Obi-Wan nodded. He climbed aboard the largest floater. The guard behind him kept the blaster against his neck. They took off for Syndicat headquarters.

CHAPTER 12

Obi-Wan watched and waited for a chance to escape, but it was impossible. Part of his Temple training had been on patience, but it had been his worst subject.

The headquarters was swarming with guards. First, he was stripped of his armor coat and visor.

"He's not a Phindian," one of the guards said, surprised. Obi-Wan said nothing.

The other guard grabbed his lightsaber. He tried to activate it, but could not. "What is this? Some primitive weapon?"

Again, Obi-Wan said nothing.

The two guards looked at each other nervously. "We'd better take him to Weutta."

Weutta turned out to be the head of security. The irises of Obi-Wan's eyes were scanned to compare to the real Guard K23M9. Obi-Wan saw the words NO MATCH on the screen. Nothing else came up.

"So, we have no record of you, rebel," the security head said, pushing his face up to Obi-Wan's. "Who are your contacts? Why did you come to Phindar? What happened to Guard K23M9?"

Again, Obi-Wan said nothing. Weutta gave him a light jab with a force pike. Even that touch was enough to send him to his knees. His head spun, and his side was on fire from the electrifying jolt.

"I'll take this one to Baftu," Weutta said. "We're on high security. He wants to see all rebels."

Weutta roughly pushed a weakened Obi-Wan down what felt like miles of hallway. At last they reached a heavily carved, massive door. A guard nodded them through. They were in a large, completely empty room with heavy tapestries hung over the windows. Another pair of massive double doors were at the opposite end.

Weutta walked toward them and stopped. He pushed Obi-Wan down to his knees, then pressed his face down. "Wait here, slug," he growled. "And don't look up."

Keeping his face down, Obi-Wan moved only his eyes to watch Weutta as the pudgy Phindian straightened his visor and smoothed his armor coat. He cleared his throat. Obviously, even the head of security was nervous about seeing Baftu. Then he pressed a button on the side of the door.

A second later, the door swung open. An annoyed Baftu stood in the doorway of his office.

"Why have you disturbed me?" he barked, scowling.

"I have brought a rebel —" Weutta babbled quickly.

"Why do you pester me with such things?" Baftu roared.

"B-because you ordered me to," Weutta answered, his voice almost a whine.

"You disgust me. Leave the rebel and get out."

"But —"

"Excuse me, Head Slug," Baftu said in a purring, murderous tone. "Are you still here in my line of sight? Or do I need to impale you on an electro-jabber until you shake yourself to death?"

"No," Weutta whispered, and ran past a kneeling Obi-Wan to the far doors. He slipped through them and disappeared.

"Baftu!" It was Terra. Obi-Wan couldn't see her. "I'm not finished!"

Baftu turned away, not even glancing in Obi-Wan's direction. He left the door partially ajar.

Slowly, Obi-Wan crept forward, his ears straining. He called upon the Force to sharpen his senses so he could hear the two. They spoke in furious murmurs.

"I was against this alliance with Prince Beju from the beginning," Terra said. "What do we know of him? We have yet to meet him or see him. Everything is done through his intermediaries. I do not trust someone I cannot see."

"He is coming here tomorrow, Terra," Baftu said. "You will be able to look at him. Enough of this."

"And why are you thinking of expansion now?" Terra went on, ignoring him. "We should consolidate our power here on Phindar. Rebel action is growing. The people are starving. Med centers are crying for supplies. You have created too many shortages, Baftu! The people are bound to revolt."

Baftu laughed. "And what if they do? They are sick and hungry. If they can find any weapons, they are too weak to hold them for long."

"This is not a joke, Baftu!" Terra cried furiously, her voice rising.

"Ah, you're getting soft, pretty Terra," Baftu said. "But if the state of things on Phindar worries you, then why don't you handle it? You can appease the people with some extra food this week. Not a bad idea, since Beju is coming. It will distract them. Just don't give them any bacta — I've promised most of it to Beju."

"I do not trust that Prince —"

"As you have said," Baftu interrupted, "over and over again. I will handle the meeting. You handle Phindar. Now I have work to do."

"What about the rebel?" Terra asked.

"You handle it. Phindar is your responsibility now, remember?"

Obi-Wan heard clicking footsteps, then the opening and shutting of a door in the other room. Quickly, he scuttled backward on his hands and knees, then pressed his face down into his hands.

A moment later, a boot nudged his shoulder. He had not even heard Terra approach on the soft carpet.

"Head up, rebel."

He raised his head. How strange to see the friendly eyes of Guerra and Paxxi in such a cruel face.

"So, you are not a Phindian. Who are you?" Terra asked impatiently.

"A friend," Obi-Wan answered.

Terra snorted. "Not to me. You impersonated a guard. You know the penalty. Well, perhaps you do not. Perhaps your Phindian *friends* did not tell you. You will be renewed and transported off-planet."

Obi-Wan did not move a muscle, but inside he cried out. Renewed! He did not imagine this. He was prepared to withstand torture. But to have his memory gone! That was too painful to imagine.

Terra sighed. She looked weary, and Obi-Wan suddenly saw a glimpse of the girl she had been. She looked away into the distance. "Don't worry, rebel. It's not as bad as people say."

Perhaps seeing traces of Guerra and Paxxi in her features made Obi-Wan feel he could risk a question. "Do you miss your family?"

She stiffened for a moment. He expected a blow, waited for it. But instead, Terra turned to him. Her bleak gaze held a sadness that was full of empty spaces.

"How can you miss what you do not remember?" she asked.

CHAPTER 13

Qui-Gon's voice was as sharp as the edge of a vibro-shiv. "You abandoned him!"

"Not so, Jedi-Gon! He insisted!" Guerra cried. "And it happened so fast. I did not know what to do!"

"You could have stayed with him!" Qui-Gon snapped.

"But Obawan told me to take the anti-register. It was most important, he said," Guerra cried desperately.

Qui-Gon let out an exasperated breath. Obi-Wan was right. They had set out to find the device. That had to be all important.

He turned his back on Guerra and tried to compose himself. They stood hidden in the shadows outside the huge warehouse. He wanted to rush at Guerra, rush at the first Syndicat guard he saw, rush into the headquarters. His anger filled him, raw and pulsing, irrational. He was surprised at the power of it. Guerra had betrayed Obi-Wan on the mining platform. Had he done it again?

"I did not know what to do, Jedi-Gon," Guerra said helplessly behind him. "Obawan insisted it so. He said, give me your coat. He said the Force would help him. Now I see he only wanted me to obey. If I knew he would be taken away, I would have so very glad gone in his place."

Qui-Gon turned and looked into Guerra's sorrowful eyes. His instinct told him to trust the Phindian. And everything he said about Obi-Wan rang true. His Padawan had sacrificed himself in order to get the anti-register device out of the building. Qui-Gon would have done the same.

Paxxi spoke up softly. "We have a signal for Duenna in case of emergency. We could activate it. She will meet us tomorrow morning in the marketplace and tell us how Obawan is and what plans there are for him. We can arrange rescue then."

"Tomorrow is too late," Qui-Gon said. "It has to be tonight. Now. I won't leave Obi-Wan there for so long."

Paxxi and Guerra exchanged glances. "So sorry to say not so, Jedi-Gon," Guerra said. "But headquarters locks down for the night. No one can get in or out. Not even Terra and Baftu."

"What about the anti-register device?" Qui-Gon asked. "You said it could get you in anywhere."

"Yes, so," Guerra said. "Anywhere. Except headquarters after lockdown."

"Duenna will watch out for Obawan," Guerra said softly. "She will protect him as best she can."

Qui-Gon turned away again. Helpless rage filled him again. But this time it was not directed at Guerra. It was directed at himself. He should have gone with Obi-Wan and let the Derida brothers fend for themselves. But he was afraid they would not be able to get the anti-register device out of the building.

"Make the decision, make another," Yoda always said. *"Remake one past, you cannot."*

Yes, he could only go forward. And Qui-Gon knew with a heavy heart that he could not rescue Obi-Wan tonight. He could not compromise the success of his mission by attempting a rescue that was doomed to fail.

*   *   *

Obi-Wan sat in a cell barely large enough to contain him. His knees were tucked up under his chin. It was cold. The chill air against his skin was like the icy fear that gripped his heart.

Anything but this, he thought. *I can stand anything but this. I can't lose my memory!*

He would lose all his Jedi training, all his knowledge. Any wisdom he had struggled so hard to gain. Would he lose the Force as well? He would lose the memory of how to harness it.

And what else would he lose? Friendship. All the friends he'd made at the Temple. Gentle Bant, with her silver eyes. Garen, who he'd fought with and laughed with and who was almost as good as he was in lightsaber training. Reeft, who could never get enough to eat, and who would stare mournfully at his empty plate until Obi-Wan passed over some of his food. They had forged strong bonds, and he missed them. If he lost his memories of them, they would be dead to him.

Obi-Wan thought of his thirteenth birthday. It seemed so long ago now. He had never done his recollection exercise. Now he remembered how Qui-Gon had admonished him. *Yes, time is elusive. But it is best to track it down.*

Obi-Wan had not tracked it down. He had not

made the time. Now he would have all the time in the world, and nothing to remember.

He pressed his forehead against his knees, feeling the fear overwhelm him. It filled his mind with darkness. For the first time in his life, he knew what it was to lose all hope.

Then, in the midst of his cold and fear, he felt a warmth inside his tunic. He reached inside to the hidden pocket against his chest. His fingers closed around the river rock Qui-Gon had given him. It was warm!

He pulled it out. The ebony stone glowed in the darkness, giving off a crystal-like gleam. He closed his fingers around it again and felt a hum against his fingertips. The stone must be Force-sensitive, he realized.

That knowledge sent a beam of pure light into the darkness of his mind. *Nothing is lost where the Force dwells,* he remembered from the Temple. *And the Force is everywhere.*

Obi-Wan turned his mind to remembering what Guerra had told him about the memory wipe. Some very strong-minded beings are able to withstand some of the effects of the wipe. Perhaps that meant the Force could help him. For what else was the Force, but strength and light?

Obi-Wan held the stone tightly. He gathered

the Force around him like a shield. He imagined it coiling around every cell in his brain like a fortress. It would hold out against the darkness, and he would hold on to his memories.

When the door to his cell opened and the guards entered, he did not even look up.

CHAPTER 14

The marketplace was crowded the next morning, even though there was even less for sale. The desperation on the faces of the Phindians mirrored Qui-Gon's. He paced impatiently, waiting for Duenna to appear.

Finally, he could wait no longer. "I'm going to headquarters myself," he told Guerra and Paxxi grimly. "I'll find a way."

"Wait, Jedi-Gon," Guerra pleaded. "It is hard for Duenna to slip away, but she always manages it."

"And so there she is!" Paxxi cried.

Duenna threaded through the crowd toward them. She was not wearing her armor coat, but a cloak and hood. She carried a large satchel.

"Any news of Obi-Wan?" Qui-Gon asked as soon as she came up to them.

She put a hand to her heart to catch her

breath. "Headquarters is on high alert. Prince Beju arrives tomorrow —"

"What about Obi-Wan?" Qui-Gon barked impatiently.

"I am trying to tell you," Duenna said. "I have never seen them act so fast. He — he was taken to a cell."

"Where?" Qui-Gon asked urgently.

"He is there no longer," Duenna said, laying a gentle hand on his arm. Suddenly, Qui-Gon noticed that her eyes were full of pity for him. His heart fell.

"What happened?" he asked hoarsely.

"He was renewed," she said, her voice breaking. "Last night. And transported off-planet at dawn this morning."

Paxxi and Guerra peered around the corner into the room where Qui-Gon sat, eyes front, cross-legged, not moving. Duenna had to return to headquarters, so they had gone straight to Kaadi's house. Being on the streets was dangerous during the day.

As soon as they had entered the house, Qui-Gon had gone to the spare room where they slept. He sat down in the middle of the floor, not speaking. He had remained there for an hour. The brothers had left him alone for a time, but he could feel their anxious eyes on him.

Without opening his eyes, he said, "I'm not giving up. I'm forming a plan."

"Of course, Jedi-Gon," Guerra said, relief coursing through his voice. "We knew this."

"Yes so," Paxxi agreed. "We know Jedi do not give up. Although, we must admit we worried a tiny bit. It is such bad news about our friend Obawan."

Qui-Gon opened his eyes. He saw the same haunted desperation in the eyes of the Derida brothers that he felt in his heart. He had had to struggle to overcome his anger at himself. It had taken time to calm his mind. Time and again he had tried to formulate a plan, only to be filled with anguish at the thought of Obi-Wan's plight. He was rocked to the core. The thought of Obi-Wan without his memory, without his training, was unbearable.

He had failed his Padawan. He should have known the Syndicat would move fast. He should have tried to rescue him last night. Now Obi-Wan was doomed to a life so empty it made Qui-Gon shudder every time he tried to conceive of it.

What of Obi-Wan's Jedi training? All of that, lost. What would the boy become? He would still be Force-sensitive, for the Force was not dependent on memory. But how could Obi-Wan use it without the lessons of the Temple to guide him? If he discovered its power, he would have it without allegiance. Would he become a lost, neutral warrior for hire? Would he use the Force for darkness, like Qui-Gon's old apprentice, Xanatos?

He did not believe that could happen. He *would* not believe it. If Obi-Wan had lost his memory, surely he would still retain his goodness.

Yes, Qui-Gon was full of worry. But he was also heartbroken. The boy he knew was gone. The diligent boy, so curious and intent on knowledge. The quick study. The boy who wanted to learn.

Qui-Gon refused to believe that all that was gone. No. He had to hope still that somehow the memory wipe would be reversible, if he could find Obi-Wan.

"And so what are you thinking, Jedi-Gon?" Guerra asked tentatively.

"We must act tomorrow," Qui-Gon said. "We must break them wide open. What better time to act then when they are trying to impress Prince Beju? First of all, they will be distracted. And second, we can destroy their alliance with the Prince before it even begins."

"It is true so," Paxxi breathed.

"We must open the warehouses when the Prince arrives," Qui-Gon said quietly. He had formed the plan in his mind, and he believed it could be done. "Can Kaadi rally the people?"

"Yes so," Guerra said, nodding.

"That will be our diversion," Qui-Gon said. "The people will rush into the warehouses. The Syndicat will panic. There will be chaos in the streets. We will go straight to headquarters with the anti-register device. That's when we'll steal the treasury."

"In the daytime?" Paxxi asked. "But it will be dangerous. And Duenna cannot help us then."

Qui-Gon turned to look at them. His blue eyes burned across the room. "Are you with me?" he asked.

The two brothers looked at each other. "Yes, so," they said together.

CHAPTER 15

The hum of the engines underneath Obi-Wan throbbed against his skull. He had been thrown on the floor of the transport, locked into cargo hold. He kept his eyes closed. He had to keep his concentration strong. He felt completely drained. Exhausted. Sick.

But he *remembered*.

They had not broken him. They had not won.

They had entered, and he hadn't even looked up, not even when they laughed at him. He slipped the river stone into the pocket of his tunic quickly, so they would not see it and take it away. The stone kept a steady glow of heat against his heart. He had drawn strength from it. It was tangible proof that the Force was with him.

While they set up the memory-wipe droid, he had built Force walls inside himself. He had enshrined every memory, even the haziest ones. He had embraced the painful with the good.

His first day at the Temple. He had been so young, so frightened. His first glimpse of Yoda, coming forward to greet him, his heavy-lidded eyes looking sleepy. "Far to come, far to go it is," he had said. "Cold and warm, it is. Seek what you are looking for, you will. Find it here, you shall. Listen."

The sound of the fountains. The river that ran behind the Temple. The chimes that the cook had hung from a tree in the kitchen gardens. He had noticed those things then, and something in him had uncurled. He had thought, for the first time, that he could feel at home there.

A good memory.

Twin metal rods were screwed against his temples. The electro-pulsers.

The stone glowed against his heart.

A visit home. His mother. Softness and light. His father. A laugh, full-bodied, joined by his mother's, just as full, just as rich. His brother, sharing a piece of fruit with him. The explosion of sweet juice in his mouth. Soft grasses underneath his bare feet.

The droid activated the memory wipe while the guards watched. A strange sensation began in his temples and moved inward. Not pain, not quite . . .

Owen. His brother's name was Owen.

Reeft never got enough to eat.

Bant's eyes were silver.

The first time he'd drawn his lightsaber. It had glowed as he activated it. Most of the Temple students had been clumsy. He had never been clumsy. Not with his weapon. The lightsaber had always felt right in his hand.

Pain now. White-hot.

The Force was bright, too. He pictured it, golden, strong, glowing, forming a barrier around his memories.

They are mine. Not yours. I'll keep them.

The Syndicat guards were surprised to see him smile.

"Happy to see that memory go, I guess," one of them said to the other.

No, it is not going. I have it. I'm holding it now . . .

Rough linen against his hands. He clung to his mother. The end of the visit. Yes, he had wanted to go back to the Temple. It was a great honor. They knew they could not keep him from it. He wanted it so much. Yet good-bye was so painful, so hard. A soft cheek was pressed against his.

I carry you always.

The way dusk fell at the Temple. Slowly, because of all the lights and white buildings of Coruscant. Light took long to leave. That's when he'd go to the river with Bant. Bant loved the river. She grew up on a humid world. Her room was kept supplied with steam. She swam like a fish in the river. As dusk fell, the color of the water would match her eyes.

Pain. He felt sick. Consciousness was slippery. If he passed out, he would lose.

Yoda. Yoda he would not lose. *Strength you have, Obi-Wan. Patience you have as well, but find it, you must. It is there within you. Search you will, until you find and hold it. Learn to use it, you must. Learn that it will save you, you will.*

He would not lose Yoda's lessons. He created a Force barrier around them. Pain crested again, sent dizziness through him. He could not last much longer.

"What's your name?" the guard asked harshly.

Obi-Wan rolled blank, sick eyes toward the guard.

"Your name," the guard repeated.

Obi-Wan pretended to search, pretended to panic.

The guard laughed. "This one is cooked."

The droid retracted the electro-pulsers. Obi-Wan slumped to the floor.

"He'll sleep now," the guard said.

"He won't dream," the other added.

But he did.

He was hauled to his feet. A Syndicat guard leered in his face.

"Ready to face your new life?"

He kept his face blank, dazed.

"I've got money riding on this," the guard said. "You won't last three days on Gala."

Gala! Obi-Wan kept a neutral look on his face as relief surged through him. What a stroke of luck! At least on Gala he could find a way to help Qui-Gon.

He knew Prince Beju's plans. Perhaps he could find someone on Gala, one of the rival politicians running for governor, to help.

The landing ramp slid down. He could see a gray stone spaceport lined with battered starfighters. A number of checkpoints prevented anyone from entering. Obi-Wan remembered what Qui-Gon had said. The royal house had plundered the planet. Rival factions fought for control. The people were close to revolt.

"Have fun!" the Syndicat guard chortled, and gave him a push down the ramp.

A probe droid buzzed behind Obi-Wan as he made his way cautiously through the spaceport hangar. When he reached the checkpoint, the guard waved him through. No doubt the Syndicat had bribed them to let him through without a challenge. Once he hit the streets of Gala, their fun would begin. They were betting on how long he'd survive.

Obi-Wan plunged into the teeming streets of Galu, the capital city of Gala. The small probot followed behind. Obi-Wan knew he had a camera trained on him at all times. It was hard to know what to do. How would he react to such a city if he had no memory of what he knew?

The city of Galu had once been grand and impressive. But the great stone buildings were crumbling. Obi-wan could see the holes and depressions where ornaments had been stripped off the facades. Trees had once lined the streets, but now there were only twisted stumps.

The Galacians were humanoids whose pale skin had a bluish cast. Sunlight on the planet was limited, and they were often called "moon people" due to their fair, luminous skin. Obi-Wan could see evidence of poverty everywhere. While the atmosphere on Phindar was one of fear, here on Gala, Obi-Wan picked up anger.

Obi-Wan kept a confused look on his face. He stared into shop windows, trying to seem as though he'd never seen the items inside before.

He avoided looking into strangers' eyes, and wandered the streets without seeming to have a destination. All the while, however, he was heading toward the gleaming building on a hill he saw in the distance, guessing it was the grand Palace of Gala. Blue and green gemstones embedded in the towers caught the weak sunlight and made the palace seem to sparkle.

Suddenly, a gigantic Galacian man blocked his path. "You," he said, placing a meaty hand on Obi-Wan's shoulder. "Do you know what I told myself when I woke up this morning?"

The probot buzzed around Obi-Wan. He resisted the temptation to react as a Jedi. He would not look into the man's eyes with clear steady courage. He would not speak firmly but respectfully in an attempt to defuse the situation. He must react in fear and confusion.

And hope he didn't get killed.

Obi-Wan let apprehension show on his face. "What?" he answered.

The huge man squeezed his shoulder painfully. "That I would slit the throat of the first hill person I saw."

"I-I'm not a hill person," Obi-Wan said. Then he realized that without memory he wouldn't *know* if he were a hill person. He pretended to look suddenly confused.

"You look like one," the Galacian said. He reached for the vibro-shiv hanging on his belt. Obi-Wan heard it leave the sheath with a slithering noise. The blade sounded very long.

Obi-Wan's hand instinctively moved toward his lightsaber. But of course he didn't have one — the Syndicat had confiscated it. And he would tip off the probot camera if he used it, anyway.

"People say I look like one," he said quickly. "All the time. I just don't understand it."

The man frowned. "You don't?"

"Because I may be ugly, but I'm not *that* ugly," Obi-Wan said. He had no idea what a hill person was. Or what they looked like. But he knew that the only way to talk his way out of this was to make friends with his enemy.

The large man stared at him blankly. Then he threw back his head and laughed. His hand dropped from Obi-Wan's shoulder.

Obi-Wan took a step back, smiling along with the man's laughter. He began to edge away. Still laughing, the man tucked his vibro-shiv back into his belt and walked on.

He kept a look of fright and confusion on his face for the benefit of the probot. He had to lose the droid, he realized. If he had to rely on his wits to survive, he'd be dead by sunset.

That thought made Obi-Wan begin to smile,

but he quickly masked it by coughing into his hand. He ducked down a side street. While he walked, he used the Jedi technique of looking without seeming to look. He gathered information, waiting for his chance.

Ahead, a cart loaded with vegetables was standing outside a café's kitchen door. A cook stood outside, arguing with the driver. Obi-Wan saw a speeder bike turn the corner ahead. This could be his chance.

He quickened his pace. When he got closer to the cart, he stumbled, keeping the dazed, confused expression on his face. His fall sent him squarely in the path of the speeder bike. He saw the driver's surprised expression before the driver turned the bike quickly to avoid running over Obi-Wan. He sideswiped the cart, which overturned. The driver of the cart began to scream at the speeder bike rider, who gunned the motor and kept on going.

The cart driver pursued him, picking up vegetables as he ran and throwing them at the speeder. One of the vegetables hit the probot, which let out a warning beep and swerved in the air. Obi-Wan quickly rolled behind the cart, then ran, doubled over, into the kitchen of the café. He darted past a surprised worker stirring soup and ran into the café itself. He headed for the door and ran out into the street. Quickly, he ducked into the shop next door.

A moment later he saw the probot fly out the door. It hovered on the street, revolving slowly. The camera scanned the passersby. Obi-Wan stayed hidden in the shop. Slowly, the probot began to cruise the street, revolving carefully. Obi-Wan quickly faded back into the store, then ran by the surprised shop owner and left by the alley exit.

The palace of Gala wasn't far. Obi-Wan hesitated at the ornate jeweled gates, wondering what to do. He could hardly walk in and announce himself. He assumed that the various ministers and candidates for the governorship must come to the palace for meetings about the upcoming elections. Should he just stop the next important-looking person and tell him why he was there?

Obi-Wan wished Qui-Gon was with him. The Jedi Knight would know what to do. Obi-Wan's mind was too filled with possibilities and guesses. He felt exposed here on the street outside the palace. He was afraid the probot would return at any moment.

Still wondering how to proceed, Obi-Wan drifted back to stand underneath the shadow of a building overhang. He watched as a small passenger spaceliner glided down from the sky. It seemed to be heading straight toward him. Obi-Wan tensed, then realized he was standing next to a small spaceport hangar.

He moved forward, still keeping in the shadow of the overhang, to watch the ship land. The ramp lowered, and a pilot got out. Someone moved forward to greet him. It was a young man dressed in a long cloak and a wrapped headdress.

"I have been waiting for three minutes," the boy snapped as the pilot approached him.

"My apologies, my Prince. Equipment check took a bit longer than usual. But we are ready to fly."

Obi-Wan stiffened. It must be Prince Beju!

"Don't bore me with the obvious," the Prince snapped. "Are my supplies loaded?"

"Yes, my Prince. Is your royal guard ready to board?"

"Don't bore me with questions — just obey me!" Prince Beju ordered. "I expect takeoff in two minutes. I will be resting during the flight, so do not disturb me."

Prince Beju flung his cloak behind a shoulder and stalked off. It was clear to Obi-Wan that the Prince must be heading to Phindar for the meeting with the Syndicat. Should he prevent the Prince from leaving?

No, Obi-Wan thought. He would just end up in prison, this time on Gala, if he interfered here. Better to stow aboard and see if he could get back to Phindar.

Obi-Wan watched as Prince Beju disappeared up the exit ramp. He was surprised to see that Beju wasn't that much older than he was. He was the same height as Obi-Wan as well, and had the same sturdy frame . . .

The idea flashed into Obi-Wan's mind like a powered-up lightsaber. Was it too risky? Should he attempt it?

He had only minutes to decide. Cautiously, he slipped onto the ship. Prince Beju was nowhere in sight. Obi-Wan realized that the Prince's transport was a small spaceliner that had been converted for his royal use. It was fitted with every luxury. Prince Beju was probably in his stateroom, behind the gilded door immediately to Obi-Wan's right.

Obi-Wan quickly went into the cockpit. He sat for a moment, familiarizing himself with the controls. He had piloted cloud cars and airspeeders and once, a huge transport ship. This shouldn't be too hard.

He headed back into the stateroom again and opened a closet door. One held supplies, but he found what he was looking for in the next — a row of headdresses similar to the one the

Prince wore. Obi-Wan quickly slipped one on his head, then wrapped a deep purple cloak in a rich fabric around his shoulders.

He returned to the cockpit and sat in the pilot seat. He saw the pilot heading for the ship, along with three royal guards. Quickly, Obi-Wan deactivated the exit ramp and started the ion engines. The pilot looked up, startled.

Obi-Wan could see the puzzlement on his face. The Padawan had counted on the fact that the headdress and cloak would confuse the pilot and guards. They would assume that Prince Beju was piloting the ship. Not for long, perhaps — but if Obi-Wan were lucky, he would have enough time to take off.

The comlink suddenly blared to life. "Two minutes are up!" Prince Beju barked. "Why are we not taking off?"

"Immediately, my Prince," Obi-Wan said crisply. He started preparations for takeoff. The ion engines revved. The pilot and the guards moved closer, trying to get a better look. Obi-Wan saw one guard's hand move to his blaster.

"Now," he muttered, and the ship blasted out of the hangar.

The coordinates for Phindar were already entered into the navi-computer. Obi-Wan piloted the ship safely out of the atmosphere of Gala. He waited until they were in deep space. Then he tossed the headdress and cloak aside, for the moment.

A weapons cabinet was mounted on the wall of the cockpit. He selected a blaster. Then he made his way back to the Prince's stateroom.

The Prince was reclining on a sleep couch when he entered. "I said I didn't want to be disturbed!" he snapped, not looking up.

Obi-Wan walked closer. He placed the blaster under the Prince's chin. "So sorry."

The Prince twisted around to look at Obi-Wan. "Guards!" he screamed.

"They decided to stay on Gala," Obi-Wan said.

"Get off of my ship!" Prince Beju blustered. "I'll see you dead! Who are you? How dare you!"

"Don't bore me with questions," Obi-Wan said, hauling the Prince to his feet. "Just obey me."

CHAPTER 16

Qui-Gon, Paxxi, and Guerra found a place to hide behind a pile of repair equipment in the Syndicat hangar. They had found out from Duenna when the Prince was scheduled to arrive. Baftu and a troop of assassin droids and Syndicat guards waited on the landing platform.

The Derida brothers and Qui-Gon wore their stolen Syndicat armor coats. Even though the coats gave them some protection, it was better to keep out of sight.

Kaadi had entered enthusiastically into their plan. She, too, thought the Prince's visit would be a perfect time to strike. She had contacted her rebel operatives. All they would need was a signal from her when the warehouses were open. She had designated people to find weapons and distribute them, find food, find supplies. And when the bacta was loaded onto the Prince's ship, she would make sure that the Phindians saw it happen.

Qui-Gon couldn't imagine the fury of a people deprived for so long of what they needed to live. Surely the capital would explode. That would give them plenty of diversion to break in and steal the treasury. Once the Syndicat was destroyed, peace could return to Phindar at last.

So why was he so uneasy? Qui-Gon wondered. Perhaps it was because the plan seemed so simple, yet was so dependent on their guesses. What if the Prince went to the headquarters first? What if Baftu double-crossed him and withheld the bacta? What if Paxxi's anti-register device didn't work? Qui-Gon had tested it on a security lock of Kaadi's, but what if the warehouse locks were different? It would have been dangerous to test it first, but should they have tried?

Perhaps he was allowing his worry about Obi-Wan to interfere with his judgment. He was anxious to bring about the Syndicat collapse so that he could find his Padawan. But was he acting rashly?

"You are worrying, Jedi-Gon," Guerra whispered. "You should not. Everything will be smooth. Paxxi and I have always been lucky."

Qui-Gon had certainly not seen any evidence

to support this. But Guerra was trying to be helpful, so he nodded in thanks.

"Yes so, we guarantee this," Paxxi added in a whisper. "The Syndicat will be weakened, maybe collapse, and Prince Beju will take off with no bacta and no alliance. Just so!"

"There is the ship!" Guerra hissed.

The Prince's ship came into view, sleek and white. It glided to a perfect landing. The ramp slowly lowered. Qui-Gon tensed. Now everything would begin.

The Prince slowly walked down the ramp alone. First, Qui-Gon was surprised. He had assumed the Prince would arrive with a royal guard.

Then he felt a rush of familiarity. But why? It took him several long seconds to realize that it was Obi-Wan in disguise.

Joy filled his heart. His Padawan was alive!

But quickly, joy was followed by confusion. Had Obi-Wan lost his memory and somehow become mixed up in affairs on Gala? That would be an incredible coincidence. How had he met Prince Beju?

"Look at him," Paxxi said in disgust. "You can tell the brute is evil."

"Look closer. That boy is Obi-Wan," Qui-Gon murmured.

Paxxi gasped. "Yes so, I thought he seemed

handsome and brave," he added quickly. "And what royal bearing he has!"

"Obawan! I am overjoyed!" Guerra exulted, his voice a whisper. Then his face fell. "But what can we do, wise Knight Jedi-Gon? We can't follow our plan now. If we alert the people that the Prince is taking the bacta, we will put Obi-Wan in great danger."

"Do you think Obawan has been memory-wiped?" Paxxi whispered. "What if the Syndicat is using him?"

"I don't know what to think," Qui-Gon said quietly, his eyes on Obi-Wan as the boy greeted Baftu.

There was only one thing he could do. Qui-Gon concentrated and reached out to the Force. He gathered it in, then directed it toward Obi-Wan like a cresting wave.

He waited, every muscle tense, every cell on alert. His heart cried out for his Padawan to hear him.

He felt Obi-Wan catch the Force and send it back to him. It broke over him like a glorious waterfall.

Qui-Gon closed his eyes in sweet relief. "It is all right," he told Paxxi and Guerra. "He has withstood the memory wipe."

Paxxi and Guerra exchanged stunned glances.

"No one has ever done this completely," Paxxi said.

"I knew he could," Guerra affirmed. "Not so, I lie. I feared for my great friend Obawan. And now I feel relief and joy."

"Me as well, good brother," Paxxi said. The two brothers looped their long arms around each other and hugged, their faces close together and smiling.

But Qui-Gon was worried. Guerra was right. They could endanger Obi-Wan with their plan. But did Obi-Wan have his own plan? Had the boy gotten himself into deeper trouble?

Qui-Gon sighed. He would have to wait. He must take no action until he knew what Obi-Wan had in mind.

One of the Jedi lessons Qui-Gon had impressed upon the boy again and again was the necessary activity of waiting. Activity can endanger, he had told him. To wait and to watch is the more difficult task, yet it is one we must master.

If only he had taught himself the lesson as well.

Obi-Wan felt the Force hit him like a wave. The knowledge that Qui-Gon was near gave him courage.

He had worried that Terra might change her

mind and appear on the platform to greet Prince Beju. She would recognize him instantly, he was sure. And though he had locked the Prince in storage in the cargo hold, he worried that the Prince would be able to make enough noise to carry beyond the ship. He needed to get Baftu away as quickly as possible.

"Welcome, Prince Beju," Baftu said as he approached. "I'm surprised to find you alone. Did you pilot yourself?"

"I thought it best to come alone," Obi-Wan said in a loud voice, hoping that Qui-Gon could hear. "I must confess that I have doubts about this alliance."

Baftu's smile faded. "But we have agreed on all terms."

"Yes, but I risk more than you," Obi-Wan said. "You make grand claims that I must trust you can fulfill. You speak of goods that I have not seen." Obi-Wan waved a hand. "You talk of bacta supplies, of a great treasury you will share to help me win back Gala. But I have not seen them."

Baftu's smile was strained. "But of course you shall. To headquarters, then. We can take refreshment, and —"

"No. The bacta first," Obi-Wan interrupted sharply.

"But I have prepared a feast," Baftu said. "We

can go over details. Wasn't it you who said you would need refreshment after the journey?"

"Do not bore me with questions!" Obi-Wan snapped. "Just obey me. The bacta first. Then, the treasury. Or I will get back on my ship and return home."

Baftu's annoyance was visible. "Did we not agree that it would be better to load the bacta under cover of darkness? If my people see the amount of bacta we have, it could be dangerous for both of us."

Obi-Wan flung the cape over his shoulder. "Can you not control your people, Baftu? Are you afraid of them? This makes me uneasy."

For a moment, Obi-Wan thought that Baftu would strike him down. But the alliance was all important to him. Baftu's small, cunning eyes narrowed, and he forced a smile. "As the Prince wishes, of course. Let us load the bacta."

"Excellent," Qui-Gon said to Guerra and Paxxi in a low voice. "Obi-Wan is stalling for time. We'll have to change our plan. First the treasury, then the warehouses. Alert Kaadi that the Prince will be loading the bacta. And then, follow me."

CHAPTER 17

Paxxi and Guerra tried their emergency signal to get Duenna's help, but after waiting a few minutes, Qui-Gon determined that they would have to get inside Syndicat headquarters without her.

"But how, Jedi-Gon?" Guerra asked. "Blast our way in? Create a diversion?"

"Let's hope there's some confusion since the Prince is here. Things won't be routine. So we'll just walk in," Qui-Gon said, lowering his dark visor.

They strode past the guard with a nod. The second one was harder. He asked for their order number.

"Prince Beju has changed plans. He wants to load the bacta first," Qui-Gon answered. "Baftu has sent us here."

"Without an order number?" the guard asked skeptically.

"Yes, we'll go on in," Qui-Gon said, bringing the Force to bear on the Phindian.

"Yes, go on in," the guard said, waving them through.

The security beams were turned off on the rear entrance, most likely because so many guards were going in and out. They were not challenged as they made their way down the halls toward the staircase to the lower level.

Qui-Gon led them to the secret room and activated the wall shift. Quickly, they headed for the security door.

"Now it's your turn," Qui-Gon said to Paxxi. He fervently hoped that Paxxi's device would work.

Paxxi jacked into the security panel. Qui-Gon heard a series of electronic beeps. Then he pressed his thumbprint against the transfer register. A beep followed. Then the light turned green, and the door opened.

"It worked, good brother!" Guerra cried. Qui-Gon wished he didn't sound quite so surprised.

The room was filled with treasures. Gems, spice, currencies, rare metals.

"We'll need transport," Qui-Gon said. "We can't get all this out of the building, so we'll have to hide it."

Paxxi and Guerra hurried back to the holding

pen at the staircase to get the floaters they'd hidden there. Qui-Gon stacked the materials. Then they all loaded them onto the floaters and took them to the supply closet. The closet could barely hold everything, but they were able to shut the door.

"Now we have to get to the warehouses," Qui-Gon said.

Paxxi closed the security door and reset the transfer register. They quickly left the secret room and closed the wall again. They hurried up the stairs and took the back entrance.

As they rounded the corner of the grand mansion toward the front gates, Qui-Gon held up a hand. "Wait," he murmured.

Baftu's gold speeder pulled up. Baftu and Obi-Wan emerged, followed by the assassin droids.

"It is better to let my guards load your ship," Baftu was saying to the boy he thought was the Prince. "They will do it quickly and efficiently, I assure you. Now you will view the treasury."

"I am pleased," Obi-Wan replied.

"You see, Jedi-Gon?" Paxxi whispered. "Our plan is working."

"We are lucky brothers," Guerra agreed.

Just then, Terra emerged from Syndicat

headquarters. She started down the stairs. Obi-Wan reached behind him to draw his cloak up around his face, but it was too late.

Terra pointed. "You are not Prince Beju!" she cried.

CHAPTER 18

Obi-Wan's mind worked quickly. Terra had recognized him. But it was still her word against his. He would have to bluff his way through.

He turned to Baftu. "Who is this who dares to challenge me?"

"My partner, Terra," Baftu said. "What are you saying?" he asked Terra fiercely. "You have never met the Prince."

"This man is a rebel," Terra insisted, drawing her blaster. "I ordered his memory wipe myself."

In the shadows, Qui-Gon's hand went to his lightsaber. Paxxi and Guerra drew their blasters, prepared to fight. They followed Qui-Gon's lead, waiting to see what Obi-Wan would do.

"If I resemble some petty criminal on your world, that is not my affair," Obi-Wan said contemptuously. He narrowed his eyes as he looked at Baftu. "Is this a ruse to deflect me from inspecting your treasury? I am already unsure about this alliance. . . ."

"No, no," Baftu soothed. "Do not listen to my partner. Let us go down to the vault."

Obi-Wan nodded shortly.

"I'm coming, too," Terra said grimly.

"What shall we do, Jedi-Gon?" Guerra whispered. "Danger is not past for Obawan."

Qui-Gon had already decided. "Paxxi, go to the warehouses with your device and open them. We must proceed with the plan. Contact Kaadi and start distributing food and weapons." Qui-Gon put a hand on Paxxi's shoulder. "I know you want to stay and help Obi-Wan. But a diversion will help him more than you can here."

Paxxi nodded and fled.

"Guerra, come with me," Qui-Gon said.

They attached themselves to the rear of the group with Baftu and Obi-Wan.

"Terra is excitable," Baftu said to Obi-Wan. "Do not listen to her."

"So you have an excitable partner who is not to be listened to," Obi-Wan said. "That does not sound wise."

Terra drifted closer to them. When Baftu turned to give an order to a droid, she murmured in Obi-Wan's ear, "No matter what Baftu thinks, I know you're a fake. I don't know how you resisted that memory wipe, but I'll find out. And I'll kill you in a heartbeat."

"Only droids downstairs," Baftu ordered briskly as they approached the stairs to the storage room. "Guards, wait here."

Qui-Gon and Guerra waited until the group was all downstairs. Then they crept after them, keeping out of sight.

Baftu activated the sliding wall. They entered the sanctuary. Qui-Gon and Guerra hovered outside, waiting. They peered inside the crack in the wall as Baftu pressed his print against the transfer register. The security door opened.

They heard Baftu's cry of dismay. Terra rushed forward.

"What is this?" she exclaimed. "Where is the treasury?"

Baftu turned to her. His face was a mask of rage. "Now I see why you were against this meeting. And why you accused the Prince of being an imposter. You had already stolen my treasure!"

"*Your* treasure! It is as much mine as yours!" Terra said angrily.

"So you admit that you stole it," Baftu said. His voice had dropped to a low, threatening tone.

"Of course I didn't steal it!" Terra said, exasperated. "Something is going on here, Baftu. This Prince is an imposter. Someone is trying to discredit me, or you — listen to me!"

Baftu turned. He nodded at the assassin droids.

It happened before anyone could move, or even blink. The assassin droids fired their built-in blasters at Terra. There was a moment where she stood, her expression blank and uncomprehending.

"You fool," she said to Baftu, and fell.

Baftu stepped over her body as though it was stray garbage on the street. He placed his hand on Obi-Wan's elbow. "Come, Prince Beju. I have taken care of the traitor. It is a matter of time before I find where she hid the treasury. This is nothing. It will not interfere with our plans."

Qui-Gon had to pull at a shocked Guerra to get him to fade back into the next room. They waited there while Baftu left with Obi-Wan and the assassin droids. They could hear Baftu still reassuring Obi-Wan as they walked away.

As soon as they were out of sight, Qui-Gon and Guerra rushed into the sanctuary. Terra lay in the doorway of the treasury room.

Guerra knelt next to her. Tenderly, he reached one long arm underneath her body and raised her to cradle her against him.

Terra looked up at him. The light in her bright

orange eyes was fading. "You don't remember me," Guerra said brokenly.

Terra's eyes cleared. For a moment, they blazed brightly as memory rushed back. "Not so, brother," she said softly. She reached up a trembling hand and touched Guerra's cheek. "Not so."

Her eyelids fluttered closed. She curled one arm around Guerra's neck, rested her head against him, and died.

CHAPTER 19

They heard a cry behind them. Qui-Gon turned. Duenna stood in the doorway, her hand at her heart.

"My good mother," Guerra said, his orange eyes full of tears. "Our Terra is gone."

Duenna knelt beside her daughter. Guerra put Terra in her arms.

Qui-Gon touched Guerra's shoulder. "We must go, my good friend," he said. "If a battle begins, Obi-Wan will be in great danger. Your people will think he's taking all the bacta."

Duenna looked at her son as she cradled Terra. Her eyes were clear. "Yes so, my son. You must go. Your sister must not die in vain."

Qui-Gon only paused to lift Obi-Wan's lightsaber from the weapons rack near the door. They hurried through the streets toward the warehouses.

They heard the commotion from blocks away. Blaster fire and shouting punctuated what sounded like one continuous roar of rage. Qui-Gon and Guerra began to run.

As they drew closer, they began to see Phindians, their arms full of supplies, rushing past them. Qui-Gon knew the plan Kaadi had devised. She had designated runners to deliver food and medicine to the sick and restock the hospitals with med supplies.

They rounded the last corner to the warehouses. Qui-Gon saw in a quick glance that Paxxi and Kaadi had done their work well. They had passed out weapons to the rebels, who held a line of resistance against the Syndicat guards. Behind that line, Phindians passed supplies from hand to hand, passing the supplies to runners who took off with them.

He saw Paxxi toss a proton grenade into a sea of Syndicat guards. Kaadi ran forward with a force pike and attacked a guard trying to blast a runner with her hands full of medpacs.

Qui-Gon quickly made his way to Paxxi's side. "Have you seen Obi-Wan?"

Paxxi shook his head. "Maybe he is by his ship."

But then Qui-Gon saw him in the midst of the Syndicat guards. Baftu stood nearby, watching the battle. Qui-Gon watched as Obi-Wan slipped a blaster from a guard's holster without his noticing. Qui-Gon sent out the Force to his Padawan, and Obi-Wan looked over the crowd straight at him. He nodded.

Qui-Gon powered up both lightsabers. They arced green and blue, glowing in the gray air. Obi-Wan leaped forward over the Syndicat guards. Qui-Gon tossed his Padawan's lightsaber high in the air. It revolved slowly, turning in a graceful arc. Obi-Wan reached out his hand and the hilt of the lightsaber landed in his palm. As he landed, he slashed out at the front line of Syndicat guards. Baftu gaped at Obi-Wan, frozen with shock to see the boy he knew as Prince Beju on the attack.

"Kill him!" he screamed at the guards.

Qui-Gon was already moving forward himself, adding to Obi-Wan's assault with his own frontal attack. They now knew where the Syndicat guards were vulnerable, and they did not waste time directing blows at their armor. Instead, they slashed out at ankles and necks, and managed to flip off the armored visors so they would have clear shots to disable them.

The Force was around them, guiding them. Obi-Wan felt its power as it battled against the dark side of the cruel Syndicat guards. He felt the good energy of the Phindians at his back, helping him. He harnessed the good and let it drive him. His blows landed where he aimed, and he evaded blaster fire with the help of the Force, which told him when to twist, move, leap, and block.

The success of the Jedi empowered the Phindians. They surged forward, crying in rage. Qui-Gon saw Baftu suddenly pale as the line of Syndicat guards broke. Guerra was the first to leap forward, a blaster in one hand and a bowcaster in the other. He drew back the bow of the bowcaster, and the laser shot out, straight at Baftu.

Baftu cried out and grabbed a Syndicat guard. He blocked the blow with the guard, who fell. Baftu turned and ran, with Guerra in pursuit.

Obi-Wan leaped over a pile of fallen Syndicat guards and took off after Baftu and Guerra. Qui-Gon evaded a blow from a force pike easily and swiveled, looking for Paxxi.

He spotted Paxxi and Kaadi off to his right. They had been surrounded by Syndicat guards with electro-jabbers. Qui-Gon cut down a guard heading toward him and leaped high over whoever was in his way. He hit the ground and used the momentum to leap up onto a partially collapsed wall.

But he was too late. A Syndicat guard jabbed

Paxxi, whose arm went numb, and he dropped his blaster. Kaadi rushed to help Paxxi as another guard fired.

The blaster fire hit Kaadi, and she fell. With his good arm, Paxxi threw the anti-register device he held at the guard. Blaster fire hit the device, causing it to ricochet back at the guard. Qui-Gon leaped into the fray, his lightsaber humming. He struck the killing blow at the guard, then turned to the next. Together, he and Paxxi finished off the rest of the guards.

Paxxi knelt by Kaadi.

"Don't look so sad," Kaadi said weakly. "I'm still alive."

Qui-Gon quickly tossed two blasters to Paxxi. "Stay with her," he told him.

Quickly, he turned and ran. He found a medic who was distributing supplies and directed her back toward Paxxi and Kaadi. Then he headed for the spaceport.

When he reached it, Baftu was surrounded by assassin droids and Syndicat guards. Prince Beju's ship stood, half loaded with bacta. While the guards protected Baftu, Phindians hurriedly unloaded the bacta from the cargo hold under fire. More and more armed rebels appeared to cover the line of those unloading bacta. Guerra and Obi-Wan were in the thick of it. Qui-Gon saw the blue glow of Obi-Wan's lightsaber slashing and jabbing as the boy moved, evading blaster fire.

Qui-Gon hurried to support Obi-Wan. But before he could strike a single blow, Baftu suddenly turned and dashed toward the entry ramp of the ship.

"He's trying to escape!" Guerra shouted. He turned to the guards. "You see where your leader's loyalty lies — with himself only!"

Baftu stumbled as he reached the ramp. The Syndicat guards turned. The closest one tackled Baftu and brought him down. They both rolled to the bottom of the ramp.

Guerra hurried forward. He placed his blaster against Baftu's head. "I arrest you in the name of the Phindian people," he cried.

"Kill the rebel!" Baftu screamed at the guards.

The Syndicat guards exchanged glances. Their arms dropped to their sides.

"Destroy him!" Baftu screamed again, this time to the assassin droids.

But Obi-Wan and Qui-Gon leaped as one from opposite ends. Lightsabers flashing, they cut the droids down like twigs.

Ion engines suddenly roared to life. The ship began to move.

"Prince Beju," Obi-Wan said. "He must have escaped from the cargo hold."

The ship rose slowly, jerkily, into the air.

"Let him go," Qui-Gon said. "His fate lies elsewhere."

CHAPTER 20

The following week, Obi-Wan, Qui-Gon, Paxxi, and Guerra stood in the town market. Around them the same stalls that had been empty so long were heaped with abundance. Supplies, fresh fruit, circuits for navi-computers, bedding, blankets. Phindians milled about with baskets on their arms brimming with fresh food and flowers.

Yoda had asked the Jedi to remain on Phindar until the provisional government had been set up. The process had taken a few days to arrange. Currently, a coalition of former council members and the last official governor of Phindar were running the planet's affairs. Elections were planned for the following month for the next official governor.

Baftu and his top lieutenants were being held in a high-security prison awaiting trial. Most of the Syndicat guards had been memory-wiped by Baftu, and some had been returned to their families in hopes that love and care would restore any memories remaining.

Obi-Wan and Qui-Gon had met the Derida brothers in the marketplace in order to view Paxxi's monument. He had destroyed the memory-wipe droid and mounted the scraps on a pedestal for all Phindians to see. They shuddered at the sight of it, and were fervently glad it had been dismantled for good.

"It was an excellent idea, good brother," Guerra said to Paxxi. "Evil must be faced in order to be conquered."

"Yes so, good brother," Paxxi agreed.

"How is Kaadi?" Qui-Gon asked. "Better, I hope."

Paxxi grinned. "Already ordering her medics around. She will be back home at the end of the week."

Guerra glanced around the marketplace, a look of sudden sadness on his face. "I am content," he said. "Not so, I lie. So much evil has been conquered, yes. But on this day I hoped also to have Terra with us as she was."

"She died as she once was, good brother," Paxxi said, his face a mirror of Guerra's sadness. He slung his long arm around his brother.

Guerra did the same. They faced each other and sighed.

"We are sad, yet not so," Guerra said.

"Yes so," Paxxi said. "Our world is free, and we have the wise Jedi-Gon and brave Obawan to thank."

"There's only one problem," Obi-Wan said. "Now that there is plenty for all again on Phindar, there's no black market. What will you do?"

"Excellent point, Obawan," Guerra said. "I, too, have wondered this. Especially since my good brother destroyed the anti-register device."

"He saved Kaadi's life," Qui-Gon pointed out.

"Just so," Guerra admitted. "Yet the sale of the device would have brought us great riches."

"It would have brought about your downfall," Obi-Wan said. "There was evil surrounding that device. You were able to use it for good. But most would not."

"As usual, you are most wise, Obawan," Guerra admitted with a sigh. "Yet it was so much fortune to lose."

"And we still do not know what we shall do," Paxxi said. "We have been rebels so long, and thieves even longer. There is no place for us here on our beloved world."

Qui-Gon looked amused. "I wouldn't say that.

What about the upcoming elections? Phindar will need a new governor. You two are heroes at the moment. Why doesn't one of you run for the post?"

Guerra laughed. "Me, governor? Ha, I laugh at Jedi-Gon's joke! I would make such a terrible politician. Wait, I lie! I would be magnificent!"

"You would be the better governor, good brother," Paxxi said. "Wait, I lie as well! I would be the better! I shall run!"

"Well, you'll have to decide between yourselves," Qui-Gon said. "It is time for us to part. Obi-Wan and I must get to Gala."

"I will take you!" Paxxi cried. "It would be my happiness!"

"Thank you, but we have a transport ship," Qui-Gon said. "This time, I would like to reach my destination."

Guerra reached out to clasp Obi-Wan's hands. "You are my great good friend, Obawan. If you ever need the services of the new governor of Phindar, you have only to ask."

"Yes, to ask me!" Paxxi said cheerfully.

"Not so, my good brother," Guerra said. "Me."

"Farewell," Qui-Gon said. "We will meet again, I'm sure."

The brothers said good-bye by wrapping their long arms around the two Jedi at once and